STAVISKY . . .

STAVISKY...

Text by Jorge Semprun
for the film by Alain Resnais
Translated from the French by Sabine Destrée
Photo editor: Jeannette Seaver

A Richard Seaver Book

The Viking Press   New York

Le "Stavisky" d'Alain Resnais
© Éditions Gallimard, 1974
English language translation Copyright © 1975 by The Viking Press, Inc.
Introduction Copyright © 1975 by Richard Seaver
All rights reserved

A Richard Seaver Book/The Viking Press
First published in 1975 by The Viking Press, Inc.
625 Madison Avenue, New York, N.Y. 10022

Published simultaneously in Canada by
The Macmillan Company of Canada Limited

Printed in U.S.A.

Library of Congress Cataloging in Publication Data
Semprun, Jorge.
    Stavisky . . .
    (A Viking Compass book; C 595)
    Translation of Le "Stavisky" d'Alain Resnais.
    Includes a new introd. and an interview with A. Resnais by R. Seaver.
    "A Richard Seaver book."
    1. Stavisky, Serge Alexandre, 1886–1934—Drama.
I. Resnais, Alain, 1922–   II. Stavisky.
[Motion picture]
PN1997.S6597S413   842'.9'14   75–17895
ISBN 0–670–00595–9

To Gérard Lebovici

"That enormous warehouse filled with merchandise known as bourgeois society will be set ablaze by adventurers, who will, as an ultimate act, throw themselves into the flames. Potlatch, celebration, largesse: these are what will mark their end."

—Jean-Paul Sartre

Director	Alain Resnais
Executive Producers	Alexandre Mnouchkine and Georges Dancigers
Screenplay	Jorge Semprun
Photography	Sacha Vierny
Camera	Phillippe Brun
Editor	Albert Jurgenson
Sound	Jean-Pierre Ruth and Bernard Bats
Music	Stephen Sondheim
Music edited by	Georges Bacri/Pema Music
Set Design	Jacques Saulnier
Costume Design	Jacqueline Moreau
Costumes (for Anny Duperey)	Yves Saint-Laurent
(for Claude Rich)	F. Smalto
(for others)	Breslave
Production Manager	Alain Belmondo
Production Companies	Ariane Films/Cérito Films (France) and Euro-International (Italy)

Cast:

Alexandre Stavisky (Serge Alexandre)	Jean-Paul Belmondo
Arlette Stavisky	Anny Duperey
Baron Raoul	Charles Boyer
Albert Borelli	François Périer
Juan Montalvo de Montalbon	Roberto Bisacco
Dr. Mézy	Michel Lonsdale
Inspector Bonny	Claude Rich
Gaston Henriet	Gigi Ballista
Inspector Boussaud	Marcel Cuvelier
Grammont	Pierre Vernier
Blackmailer	Michel Beaune
Inspector Gardet	Van Doude
Laloy	Guido Cerniglia
Erna Wolfgang	Silvia Badesco

Michel Grandville	Jacques Spiesser
Gauthier	Maurice Jacquemont
Deputy Véricourt	Jacques Eyser
Van Straaten	Fernand Guiot
Édith Boréal	Nike Arrighi
Chairman of the Stavisky *Commission*	Daniel Lecourtois
Police Archive Employee	Samson Fainsilber
Young Man *(the matriscope inventor)*	Gérard Depardieu
Professor Pierre	Raymond Girard
Leon Trotsky	Yves Peneau
Natalia Trotsky	Catherine Sellers
Trotsky's Secretary	Niels Arestrup

The publishers wish to express their thanks to the American distributor of *Stavisky* . . . , Cinemation Industries, Inc., for their help and cooperation. Thanks too to Films Ariane in Paris for their help in obtaining additional photographs and documents.

CONTENTS

INTRODUCTION

by Richard Seaver

In the early part of January 1934, a man was killed in a remote section of France; at the time of his death, he was unknown to all but a handful of Frenchmen. The man's name was Serge Stavisky. The place of his death was a hilltop house at Chamonix in the French Alps. The "handful" of Frenchmen who knew him prior to January 9, 1934, included, however, top politicians, statesmen, financiers, businessmen, and a number of high-ranking police officials, including the Commissioner of Police himself. In a matter of days, Serge Stavisky's name was known the length and breadth of France, for the scandal of and surrounding his death led to the fall of at least one administration and shook the very foundations of the Third Republic.

Who was Serge Stavisky, and how did his death have such repercussions? There were, in truth, at least two Serge Staviskys: the first was born on November 20, 1886, in Slobodka, Russia. When Serge was thirteen the entire Stavisky family left Russia, emigrated to France, and obtained French citizenship. Serge's father, an excellent and hard-working dentist, soon had a flourishing practice in the Champs-Elysées section of Paris. But young Sacha seems to have taken after his paternal grandfather, who had emigrated with the family from his native Ukraine and who spent his time dreaming mad dreams and concocting wild schemes for making an easy franc. By the time he was twenty Sacha had already had one brush with the law. Enamored of the theater, and with hopes of becoming a performer himself, he had business cards printed in the name of a publisher of the period, Monsieur Lemerre, with which to obtain free tickets to the theater. The ruse was quickly unmasked, but Lemerre, fortunately for Sacha, did not press charges, and the police let him off with a simple admonishment. Two years later, however, the two schemers, grandfather and grandson, joined forces in a far more serious enterprise. Their plan was to take over the management of one of the principal theaters of Paris, the Marigny, which in 1909 lay vacant. The only thing lacking was money: but as Serge was beginning to learn, that problem should never stand in the way of any undertaking, for money was there if you only knew how to find it. As was customary in those days, theater managers would advertise in various papers for people interested in handling the concessions. Parties responding were asked to put up security, and before long the two partners had amassed twelve thousand francs, a sum sufficient for them to have actually moved ahead and put on a show. But that would have been too easy, and too honest: together, grandfather and grandson simply pocketed the money and took off for parts unknown. Within days, those who had posted security lodged complaints, an investigation was opened, and an indictment was returned against the two men. Whether or not the shock of impending arrest was too great for him remains unclear, but grandfather Stavisky resolved his problem with the law by conveniently passing away, leaving Serge to face the music alone. His reaction and his way of handling his defense give considerable insight into the man and indicate his future path. He engaged as his lawyer Albert Clemenceau, an attorney of great repute himself and, perhaps more important, the brother of Georges Clemenceau, who was then *Président du Conseil*. Serge knew, or sensed, that in France, and perhaps in any country, an accused person's best chance is a good lawyer, preferably well connected. His theory proved correct, for Clemenceau managed to obtain postponement after postponement, and the trial did not actually take place until 1912. The results? A two-week suspended sentence and a fine of twenty-five francs. Not a bad profit, considering the investment, a fact one suspects that Sacha was quick to note at the time.

In 1912 he opened in Paris an office which today would probably correspond to a public relations firm, specializing in settling business disputes, and through that office started a number of businesses of his own, none of which, however, became successful enough to keep up with his needs. But Sacha had another trump which was to serve him through the balance of his career and which, especially at this juncture, stood him in good stead: he was a vital, dashing, and good-looking young man whose seductive powers with women were considerable. When he was really down and out, he could always find bed and board—and usually pocket money to boot—with one of his mistresses. But his life at the time was a hazardous and ultimately harrowing one, for complaints from dissatisfied clients continued to flow into the police, and he must have felt constantly no more than one step ahead of the law. A police file of the period notes: "Stavisky, Serge: Con-Man extraordinary, capable of any undertaking so long as it promises to be profitable." And another: "Knows how to use with incredible ability important relations and influential contacts he has managed to cultivate in all areas." Those two observations proved absolutely accurate, not only at the time but throughout the rest of Stavisky's life. Nonetheless, all his relations and "influential contacts" had, by the time World War I broke out, brought him neither fame nor fortune, and 1914 found him a refugee in Belgium, whence he had fled to avoid a charge in Paris of breach of trust by one of his clients.

As is often the case with men of Serge Stavisky's caliber and inclinations, war offered him opportunities not always available in more stable periods. Serge joined the Foreign Legion in the summer of 1914 and served for a scant six months before being released for reasons that remain unclear. But his discharge was honorable, and the fact he had served had the added benefit of giving him amnesty for all previous charges against him.

Back in Paris, Sacha joined forces with a fairly successful cabaret singer, Fanny Bloch, and opened a clandestine casino. It was still a life one step ahead of the law, but at least now money was coming in, enough so that he and Fanny soon opened a night club on the rue Caumartin which catered to soldiers on leave. It was a huge success, and, for the first time, Serge was in possession of fair sums of money. It could have been the beginning of his dream come true, but his relations with Fanny, which had always been stormy, grew worse, and after one particularly tumultuous battle, Fanny went to the police. The couple broke up and went separate ways, but after the accounts were totaled up and divided, Sacha's share of the profits came to 800,000 francs—roughly the equivalent of $200,000, or £50,000 sterling. Not the millions he had dreamed of perhaps, but in 1920 certainly a very respectable sum; with it he could have lived comfortably if he had wanted to invest it in some legitimate enterprise. But living comfortably seems never to have been possible for Serge Stavisky; within a short time he had lost his "fortune," unwisely invested in the movie industry, about which he knew little or nothing.

The early post–World War I years found him again involved in companies that sprouted like mushrooms, and disappeared almost as quickly. There was an import-export business ostensibly importing oil but serving as a cover for more dangerous traffic; another company manufactured and sold beef bouillon cubes; there was a scandal involving the theft of a large number of securities, in which Stavisky's name was raised but no action taken against him. Was he already, at that time, benefiting from police protection? An incident in 1924 would lend further credence to that possibility: one night in a Paris *boîte* Serge persuaded a drunk American who owed him money to write him a check for 600 francs. When the following day a cohort of Stavisky's presented it for payment at the American Express, the 600 had been neatly turned into 48,200. Stavisky—or his accomplice—had neatly altered the "6" to a "482": a difference of about $12,000! When the alarm was put out for Stavisky's accomplice, a Rumanian named Popovici, the latter, on Serge's advice, fled the country. Stavisky? Free and clear. But when a few months later Popovici reappeared in Paris, he was arrested immediately. Since Serge had been virtually the only person aware of his return, Popovici became convinced it was his "friend" who had turned him in. He promptly cooperated with the police and denounced Stavisky. This time the authorities had the goods on him; but when the case came to trial, the key piece of evidence, the check itself, was missing from the file. Once again, Sacha got off scot-free; not quite, though: before his case was thrown out of court, he had, for the first time in his life, spent a few days in jail. A sobering experience? Apparently not. For his next coup was far more ambitious than any he had been involved in till then: counterfeiting treasury bonds. Through some leak, however, the police uncovered the operation and arrested several people. Stavisky? No, even though the material was discovered in a house rented in his name. He vanished from the scene for a time, while his colleagues languished in jail. When he reappeared, early in 1926, it was still as the first "Serge Stavisky," but the demise of that initial identity was not far off. For one can date the emergence of the second Serge at one of two possible junctures in his life: either in 1926, when he met the only real love of his life, Arlette, a twenty-two-year-old model who worked for Chanel; or late in December 1927, when after exactly eighteen months in the Santé prison awaiting trial for the affair of the counterfeit treasury bonds, he was freed "for reasons of deteriorating health."*

Whichever date one takes, the birth of the new Sacha was complete and undeniable: he assumed a new identity, Serge Alexandre; a new title, financial advisor; and he gave legitimacy to the son that Arlette had borne him by marrying her early in 1928.

At the age of forty, a new life was beginning for Serge Alexandre. As Serge Stavisky, he had already made and promptly lost several fortunes, but they were as nothing compared to his future aspirations. With the lovely Arlette at his side, Serge Alexandre re-emerged into the world and whirl of Paris as a wealthy businessman: he had understood that to make money on a large scale one must affect money, lavishly but tastefully; and, equally important, he had fully realized that, properly placed, money could buy almost anything, including protection in the highest echelons of power. Armed with this sure knowledge, plus what even his harshest critics acknowledged to be an undeniable intelligence and charm, Serge Alexandre founded several companies, all of which he controlled but whose various boards of directors inevitably included some of the most prestigious names in France. His sumptuous dinners and parties became the talk of the social set, and the press, always impressed by names, filled its pages with accounts and photos of his extravaganzas. Few made the connection between Serge

---

* Three days after his release, however, he celebrated New Year's Eve in a Montparnasse nightclub with Arlette and a few friends. There had been, apparently, a medical miracle.

Alexandre and Serge Stavisky, and those who did quickly dismissed the notion that there was any meaningful connection between the two identities. Only two segments of the population seemed bound not to forget: the scandal-sheet press on one hand, and the police on the other. The former could be bought off with money; the latter for the most part appeared too intimidated by Serge Alexandre's new entourage—which included cabinet ministers, deputies, ex-generals, international bankers and brokers—to move against him.

And yet the name Stavisky, foreign and Jewish in xenophobic, anti-Semitic France, could not be entirely forgotten. For one thing, Serge himself could not forget: when in April 1926 the police had come looking for him at his father's, the elder Stavisky, who had earlier warned his wayward son that the day Serge publicly dishonored the family name he, Emmanuel, would kill himself, remained true to his word. As soon as the police had satisfied themselves that Serge had not taken refuge at his father's, and had left, Emmanuel committed suicide. Then too, the charge of counterfeiting and three other charges of fraud for which he had been arrested in 1926 were still hanging over his head. Through Serge Alexandre's contacts and through medical connivance, Serge Stavisky's trial had been postponed a dozen times over a six-year period. Not until the charges had been dropped and the suit dismissed could Serge Alexandre rest easy. But that was no simple matter, as his lawyers kept pointing out, and required large sums of money to satisfy the several plaintiffs involved.

Not that money was lacking; it was simply that Sacha always managed to spend money faster than he made it. In 1930 Sacha and Arlette went through more than five million francs—well over a million dollars. Gambling took a large chunk, with entertainment a close second. In 1931 their expenditures were even higher, and even though France had as yet been relatively untouched by the Depression, times were growing increasingly difficult in Europe as well as in the United States. If anyone ever thought to ask where Alexandre's money came from—and few ever stooped to such coarseness—the answer was generally a vague shrug: "Business. He heads up several businesses, you know. Big businesses." And if indeed "le grand Serge" made money from his food company with headquarters in Cannes and his Paris-based construction companies and refrigerator company, he had, by this time, concocted one of the most gigantic frauds of all time.

In France, there exists an institution known as *crédits municipaux*, which are municipal pawnshops. They work on the same principle as any pawnshop, with the exception that, being a government institution, they can issue bonds to raise the capital necessary to lend money. Serge Alexandre was quick to see the potential in such a situation: all one needed was a corrupt, or corruptible, director. He found the man he needed in the city of Orléans, just south of Paris: the director of the Orléans Municipal Pawnshop was a man named Monsieur Desbrosses, who was open to any proposition, so long as he shared in the profits.

Serge Alexandre's idea was so simple it looked foolhardy: instead of pawning real jewelry at the Municipal Pawnshop, he would pawn fakes, but against sums equaling what would be lent against the genuine item. In the course of less than three years this system worked to perfection: more than forty million francs were lent to Serge Alexandre, against securities that were virtually worthless. But the police—or at least certain incorruptibles who had refused to forget that "le grand Serge" was, nonetheless, still at heart Sacha-the-con-man—watched and followed his moves, steadily reporting to their superiors. Wasn't it astonishing, they suggested, that such fabulous sums were lent to a single individual? Ah, but the replies came back, for a man such as Serge Alexandre, whose businesses are enormous and constantly expanding, those sums are doubtless but a drop in the ocean. And in any event, wasn't he putting up as security some of the most precious jewels in all of Europe? For, apparently, no one had figured out the "x" of the magic equation, that is that the pledged articles were but clever fakes, what Janet Flanner, reporting from Paris on the ensuing scandal, would term "spinach-colored glass." Nonetheless, suspicions were sufficiently aroused so that an investigation was undertaken. Desbrosses, who had profited royally from the scheme, was sure Serge Alexandre could never reimburse the loans, and that the game was over. But before the auditors arrived, by some magic stroke the master swindler had indeed covered the loans outstanding and withdrawn the only evidence against him— the phony pledges.

Where had he found, overnight as it were, the equivalent of some £2,500,000 pounds sterling, or $10,000,000? Quite simply, from the funds of his various other companies, and especially his Building and Loan Association, whose capital resources were impressive. But that loan too would have to be reimbursed if the company was to remain solvent for very long. If one had borrowed from Peter to pay Paul, where now would one borrow to pay Peter? The obvious answer was to find another soft touch such as he had discovered and set up in Orléans, another municipal pawnshop where he could work the same scheme, perhaps on an even larger scale. Again through connections—always through connections—Serge Alexandre settled on the city of Bayonne in southwestern France, which was doubly blessed: first, it did not have a municipal pawnshop; and second, Serge Alexandre was friends with the mayor. Within a short time, a spanking new municipal pawnshop was opened in that fair city. And who was brought in to run it? None other than Monsieur Desbrosses, whose long and exemplary experience in Orléans made him ideally suited for the post!

Thus the dance began again, but this time Serge Alexandre added a new twist: not only would the false jewels, whose values would be duly certified by another accomplice, be given in pawn against often staggering sums, but the fraud would be further compounded by doctoring the municipal bonds themselves. On a ten thousand franc bond, for example, the director would note, on the part of the bond retained for the city records, a much smaller amount, say one thousand francs: the nine thousand francs difference would go into the pockets of Serge Alexandre and those around him. By 1932 the "budget" of the Bayonne Municipal Pawnshop, then less than two years old, had reached an incredible one hundred million francs, a sum hardly commensurate with a city with a population of less than one hundred thousand. Why were suspicions not aroused? Because the new Pawnshop had the backing of the mayor and the approval of the City Council; because the bonds were considered as safe as gold; because, through another of Serge Alexandre's connections, Monsieur Dalimier, the then Minister of Labor, had written a letter of recommendation intended for banks, insurance companies, and large investors, which said in part: "Considering the security these municipal bonds offer, and most especially those in the Bayonne area, they would seem to me to be one of the safest and best investments any board of directors of financial institutions could make." Triple A? Yes, if the A's all stood for "Alexandre," for most of the enormous sums flowing out of Bayonne were going directly to him, first to reimburse the forty-three million he had "borrowed" from his own companies to seal off the Orléans' problem, then to satisfy his great and growing personal and business needs.

Con-men, it has been said, have several identifying characteristics, but high among them are these: that they enjoy the danger to which they constantly expose themselves and that they have an abiding faith that somehow the future will take care of itself—and them. Stavisky's whole career, from his juvenile theft of gold from his father's dental office to his last, monumental scheme, is like an inverted pyramid: if the occasional theft of a few grams of gold was the apex of the pyramid, the base was his last and most grandiose plan. Known as the Affair of the Hungarian Bonds, it was based on the following, again fairly simple, premise: after World War I a portion of the Hungarian population had been given indemnities, payable by the German government, in the form of long-term bonds. Now, twelve years after the Treaty of Trianon, those obligations had not been met and the bonds were considered worthless. Alexandre's plan was to buy them up for a song, use them as security—with the approval of the French Foreign Office, where, again, he had influential friends—and against that security issue new bonds for a company he planned to create: the International Monetary and Development Fund, the goal of which would be to finance large-scale construction not only in France but throughout Europe. The principle was not all that different, but the stakes were far greater: the envisioned capitalization of the new company was one billion francs! More than enough to pay off his Bayonne debts and still have plenty to carry out his future plans. For by this time, as the effects of the Depression were starting to be felt more fully in Europe, Serge Alexandre was beginning to believe his own fabrications. Doubtless conceived primarily to extricate himself from his growing financial predicament, the International Monetary and Development Fund, with its impressive board of directors and its well-appointed headquarters on the Place Saint-Georges in Paris, began to take on a new reality for its conceiver. Through it he could and would help save Europe, create tens of thousands of new jobs; everything he had done till now would be justified, not only in the eyes of society but in his own as well. Finished were the days of tight-rope walking, of hovering constantly over the abyss. The transformation from Sacha Stavisky to Serge Alexandre was complete. But not quite . . .

On the night of December 22, 1933, a call came from Bayonne. It was the director of the Municipal Pawnshop calling. The news was catastrophic: the auditors had just been there. They had discovered the fraud; no, he had revealed nothing. In fact, he had warned them they should keep what they had just discovered to themselves, for the affair was far more complex, and involved many more people, than they suspected. Serge Alexandre did his best to reassure his accomplice. He would take the necessary steps immediately. But above all, say nothing more. When, however, the police returned, arrested, and further interrogated the director, he broke down and spilled the whole story, including the identity of the person behind it: Serge Alexandre.

The rest of the Stavisky saga is much as depicted in the film by Semprun and Resnais: the flight from Paris, leaving Arlette behind; the vain attempts to cover up; the betrayals; and, finally, the death in the isolated house above Chamonix (the house shown in the film is the actual *Vieux Logis* where Stavisky was shot forty years before the Resnais re-creation), a death whose ambiguity has never been solved. Part of the ensuing scandal and political uproar was based on the fact that, while the initial report was suicide, rumors of murder to keep Serge Alexandre from talking were rife. The subsequent suspicious death of a police official who was purported to know a great deal about the Stavisky Affair added further fuel to the fire. Exactly a month after Stavisky's death, with the French population avidly devouring the daily revelations of his long list of business and political "friends"—much as the United States followed the unraveling of Watergate four decades later—a crowd formed on the Place de la Concorde. It was disorganized and leader-less: all it seemed to be sure of was that the men in power, who had so long connived and corrupted, had to be thrown out. Across the bridge, on the Left Bank, the *Chambre des députés* was in session, heatedly debating, when the crowd surged across the bridge and did battle with the police, who steadily re-treated but did not break ranks. The *députés*, seeing what was happening, quickly adjourned and dispersed. Finally the crowd was contained and, its anger spent, at least for the moment, broke up and scattered. But the pressures that had caused it to form in the first place were still present, and within a few days the government did fall.

It is doubtless significant, or at least symbolic, that the Prime Minister of that government was M. Camille Chautemps, himself what the French caustically refer to as a *fils à papa*. To make matters worse, it was his brother-in-law who had been Police Commissioner during Serge Alexandre's heyday and who, apparently, had faithfully failed to prosecute, through almost automatic postponements, the pending Serge Stavisky case over the years.

If one harks back to the inverted pyramid, it becomes clear that the image obtains to the end: for Serge Stavisky had saved his most grandiose scheme for the last, one that dwarfed even the plan for the Hungarian bonds: he had succeeded in toppling a government.

So much for the "real" Stavisky. What about the "cinema" Stavisky? As the film's author, Jorge Semprun, reminds us in his Introduction to the French edition, "any film is a fiction, even if that fiction assumes the formal structure—the dramatic mask—of a brief, of a factual file that one appears to be trying to sort out and clarify. In films, to outdo the illusion of reality in no way eliminates the reality of the illusion. The *Stavisky* written for Alain Resnais is a fiction which has a distinct relationship with historical reality. . . . And yet the task of building that fiction on the basis of what is 'real' was not easy. When one reads or listens to eye witnesses, journalists, and even historians on the subject of the Stavisky Affair, one finds oneself enmeshed in all sorts of contradictions and inaccuracies, not to mention omissions and out and out lies. . . . Fortunately, we have a means of ferreting out the truth—the uncertain, mysterious, and troubling truth—about the Stavisky Affair and its consequences: the several volumes, comprising some ten thousand pages, of the two parliamentary commissions set up in 1934, one to investigate the Stavisky case itself, the other the events of February 6th."

If, therefore, the film *Stavisky* is carefully based on facts—facts which often contradict the impassioned accounts of the periods—it is very much a fiction in that it makes no attempt simply to document the course of a troubled and meteoric life. As Alain Resnais says in the interview that serves as an epilogue to the present volume, "I have always been interested in the functioning of the human brain. Especially when there seem to be two very contradictory impulses warring within the same mind." In Serge Stavisky, to a very high degree, the life impulse was at war with the death instinct. Positive versus negative. Charm, gaiety, love, and great generosity on one hand; the constant temptation to the precipice on the other. Such a person, such a complex and contradictory mind, was doubtless what most intrigued and fascinated Resnais, whose films have all dealt, in one way or another, with the complex workings of the human mind. That is why Resnais's films are so intensely personal, why they are like those of no other filmmaker.

All of Resnais's films are the results of a very close collaboration between a writer and Resnais. Once the subject is established, the writer does an initial draft, or treatment, after which writer and director discuss it scene by scene, often line by line, in excruciating detail, until the distinction between writer and director blurs or disappears. (I know, having worked with Resnais for a year on such a script.) Resnais has an almost obsessive respect for the written word, and if asked whether he has ever written any scripts will inevitably reply, in mock or real horror: "Never! I'm incapable of putting a single line on paper." Which may be true, but only to a point. What Resnais is looking for, always, is a vision and a sensibility in a writer that closely parallels his own. And though he has used half a dozen different writers (Semprun, with *Stavisky*, is the only one he has worked with twice), each Resnais film bears so markedly his own stamp that one can say without question that the vision of writer and director have ultimately fused.

Three, four, five, or six drafts after the initial effort, Resnais is ready to break the work down into a shooting script. While the finished work can truly be said to be collaborative, many particular scenes or elements "belong" to one or the other. In *Stavisky*, for instance, the Trotsky episodes are clearly Semprun's. Any film, Semprun has said, is the result of myriad pressures, images, evocations—some having no direct relationship to the project.

When a French producer first raised the possibility with Semprun of writing a script on the Stavisky Affair, the subject, Semprun notes, evoked a number of images in his mind. He remembered, as a boy in Madrid, seeing his father come into the room one morning in February 1934 and throw the newspaper on the table as he said: "*Paris arde por los cuatros costados!*" (Paris is burning from one end to the other!). The picture on the front page depicted the riots on the Place de la Concorde and the burning bus that came to be the uprising's symbol. He remembered, too, and perhaps above all, a scene he had witnessed later that same year on Madrid's Cybele Square. A man, dressed in worker's blue, wearing espadrilles, was running for his life across the square. Silently. And the square was silent, too. At his passage, the pigeons flew from their perch on the statue of Cybele. And then an open truck of the *Guardia Civil* appeared on the square, and the men standing on the truck platform opened fire on the fleeing man. A second later he stumbled, but did not fall, doubtless hit by an initial bullet. Then a hail of bullets struck him full force and he plunged forward, one shoe flying past his blood-spattered body. And then silence again. A few seconds later, the pigeons returned to their perch on the statue. Neither of those images figures in the film; yet it is safe to say that without them, the script as Semprun conceived and wrote it would not have been the same.

Another image, or rather two images juxtaposed: the first, imagined not lived, of Trotsky and his wife arriving on the southern coast of France aboard the cutter *Neptune* one day in July 1933; and over it, the cry, seven years later, of a Trotsky mortally wounded by Ramon Mercader, in Coyoacán, Mexico: "Natacha, I love you!" the latter image darkening the earlier, sun-drenched image of the Mediterranean.

Both Semprun and Resnais were searching for images for the film, symbols to situate the period, something meaningful against which to juxtapose Stavisky's life and career. Trotsky seemed a possibility, though only one of many considered. But when Semprun discovered, in reading the report of the investigative commission, that the police inspector assigned by the Minister of Foreign Affairs to investigate Serge Alexandre late in 1933, Inspector Gangneux, was the same man assigned to watch Trotsky during part of his exile in France, he had the link he needed. "The thick, banal historical record allowed us to join dramatically the two stories—Trotsky's and Stavisky's— through a real policeman, who in the film we named Inspector Gardet. This seemingly incredible coincidence, that some might have assumed pure fabrication on the part of the scriptwriter, was actually straight out of the historical record. And that episode may serve as a concrete example of the method we generally employed in the film to insert fiction into the often obscure, and even contradictory, reality of the historical record."

One final word: at the time Semprun was exploring, at the request of the producer Gérard Lebovici, the possibility of writing a script on Stavisky, Alain Resnais was in the United States. Semprun and the producer had not settled on a director at that point, and Resnais was far from mind. And yet, as so often happens when one enjoys the advantage of hindsight, it seems impossible now, in viewing this masterful film, that any other collaboration was even conceivable.

STAVISKY . . .

NOTE

Although the script as presented here represents the "final" scenario, there were instances during the shooting itself when minor changes of sequence or emphasis were made, as often happens in the making of any film. The observant reader, for instance, will note that the sequence of some of the scenes in *Le Vieux Logis*, near the end of the film, varies slightly from the order in the picture itself, and that there is a slight but significant difference between the end as written and the end as shot. But these variations are minor and in no way affect the structure or basis of the work itself.

1.

Cassis—a town on the French Riviera. The time is 10:00 a.m., July 24, 1933.

A car is parked on the coastal road overlooking the Mediterranean. It happens that right next to the car is a sign specifying the site: CASSIS.

Three young men who have gotten out of the car look down and off to their right at the placid blue sea below. One of them, whose name is Michel Grandville, points to a motor boat which is approaching the port of Cassis.

GRANDVILLE: There they are! There they are!

Jostling one another and laughing a bit nervously, they climb back into the car.

The name of the motor boat which, on that July morning, is chugging toward the harbor is Neptune. *On the deck of the boat, leaning up against the railing, is a couple. The man, who is dressed in white linen but almost smothered in a blanket despite the bright sunshine, has a tiny white beard and appears slightly stooped. His companion, who is thin and shorter than he, is wearing a kerchief to protect her hair from the wind. She clings tightly to the man.*

*

A room in the Cassis Town Hall. Portrait of French President Lebrun on the wall, as well as a number of civic inscriptions. Chief Inspector Gardet of the Sûreté générale—the Criminal Investigation Department—is greeting the couple just glimpsed on the deck of the Neptune.

GARDET: Allow me to introduce myself: Chief Inspector Gardet, of the *Sûreté générale*.

Michel Grandville and his two companions are observing the scene.

GARDET: Monsieur Davydovich Bronstein, also known as Leon

Trotsky: the French Government, considering the very exceptional circumstances in which you find yourself and wishing to make a humanitarian gesture, grants you exile in France, it being clearly understood that you will refrain from any involvement in the internal affairs of France.

Gardet speaks quickly, with almost no break between the words, as though he were reciting from memory. Trotsky nods.

GARDET: We took the precaution of having you land here in order to avoid any political demonstration. In Marseilles, where the press is waiting for you, it would have been impossible to keep your movements a secret.

Again Trotsky nods. Inspector Gardet hands him a piece of paper.

GARDET: This is a copy of the official notice granting you permission to reside in France, Monsieur Trotsky.

*

A quiet little square, well shaded by the surrounding trees. Two cars loaded with baggage prepare to depart.

In the first car, Trotsky and his wife are seated, accompanied by two or three good and faithful followers. Inspector Gardet is traveling in the second.

A little off to one side, Michel Grandville and his two companions watch as the two cars are loaded, then as they drive off.
Now the cars are gone, and beneath the July sun the little square is deserted.

GRANDVILLE: So that's that! A page of history has been turned. Lenin's closest companion, the victor of October, the founder of the Red Army, once again goes into exile.

Trotsky's car, followed by that of the Sûreté générale, moves away down a straight road.

2.

The Hôtel Claridge in Paris. The time is 10:15 a.m., July 24, 1933.

An elevator descends and arrives at the lobby floor of the hotel.
From it emerges Serge Alexandre. He appears to be about forty, is svelte and impeccably dressed, with a carnation in his

buttonhole. The ease of his every movement, his self-assured smile, and his velvety look all bespeak a considerable and undeniable charm.

There is nothing particularly noticeable about the man who is with him. His name is Inspector Boussaud, but this we will learn only later.

As Alexandre arrives, a bellboy hurries over to him.

BELLBOY: Shall I call for your car, Monsieur Alexandre?

Alexandre smiles at him and makes a gesture with his hand.

ALEXANDRE: Yes . . . Tell my chauffeur that I'll be there in a few minutes.

Another bellboy appears.

SECOND BELLBOY: Monsieur Borelli is waiting for you in the lobby, Monsieur Alexandre, with Baron Raoul!

Alexandre smiles and shakes his hand. Then he takes Inspector Boussaud by the arm and propels him along with him as he walks.

ALEXANDER: Who is Bonny working for? That's what I really want to find out!

Boussaud's smile is ambiguous.

BOUSSAUD: Inspector Bonny sometimes works for himself!

ALEXANDRE: You have all day to ferret that out, Boussaud! If it's money he wants, that's no obstacle! All it means is one more palm to grease!

BOUSSAUD: Nine o'clock tonight, at the Place Saint-Georges. I'll let myself in by the back door.

And with those words, he leaves.

Alexandre continues on through the hotel lobby, a huge lobby surrounded by a circular gallery and crowned with stained-glass windows.

People watch him as he passes.

Alexandre is at the table where Baron Raoul and Albert

Borelli are awaiting him, both reading the morning paper—Le Matin, to be more precise.

Baron Raoul's looks, gestures, diction, and bearing are those one would expect a baron to possess in those films where barons play a part.

Albert Borelli's face is impassive, but he has a sharp eye. He is a man of few words but not of few thoughts.

ALEXANDRE: Thank you for coming back from Biarritz, Baron. I needed your good advice. I'm afraid Gaston will do something foolish if I let him make all the decisions at the Empire.

BARON RAOUL: Sacha, what a pleasure to see you! And to be of service to you.

ALEXANDRE: I want you to tell me all about Biarritz, Baron! Was Arlette still the most beautiful one there?

BARON RAOUL: Arlette is always the most beautiful one, Sacha! If only you had seen her yesterday, in our friend Montalvo's Hispano-Suiza. . . .

With these words spoken by Baron Raoul, the images he evokes in his mind flash onto the screen.

*

Biarritz. Bright sunlight. In front of the sumptuous Hôtel du Palais. The ocean lies in the background. A gleaming Hispano-Suiza moves forward toward a small crowd assembled to witness a luxury-automobile competition. The members of the jury are seated on folding chairs, Baron Raoul among them. The car is being driven by its owner, Juan Montalvo de Montalbon, a man we will come to know later. The car stops, and a beautiful woman emerges from it. Superbly graceful. Haughty and distant. She leans back against the glittering car.

BARON RAOUL (*voice over*): . . . an absolutely stunning dress, and the way she carried her head . . . a princess! The jury was . . .

ALEXANDRE (*voice over*): Later, Baron, later! I want to know every last detail.

*

With these words, we find ourselves back in the lobby of the Hôtel Claridge in Paris.

ALEXANDRE: I'm keeping you with me everywhere I go today.

As he is speaking to Baron Raoul, Alexandre notices a young woman seated at a neighboring table. A charming-looking

woman *resplendent in her summer frock. She notices that Alexandre is eyeing her. She toys with a pendant she is wearing around her neck. An antique piece of jewelry, no doubt; the camera catches the rubies that flame and sparkle in the light as they move.*

But Alexandre has turned back to his friends.

ALEXANDRE: What's new in the world?

BARON RAOUL: A strike in Hollywood . . . Wall Street as disastrous as ever.

BORELLI: Speicher won the Tour de France.

Borelli speaks in calm and measured tones.

BARON RAOUL: Did you see the article in *Le Matin* today by your friend Morel?

It is obvious that Alexandre hasn't seen the article.

BARON RAOUL: "The Call of Blood." What a melodramatic title! And do you know what blood they're referring to? Jewish blood, no less!

Borelli glances at Alexandre, to see his reaction. But if he has any reaction, Alexandre fails to show it.

Baron Raoul picks up the newspaper and begins reading Morel's article, which appears on the front page of Le Matin.

BARON RAOUL: "To protest against the racial persecutions in Germany, Lord Melchett, head of the Chemical Industries Trust in England, has renounced the Christian faith and announced that he has converted to Judaism, the faith of his ancestors. And Morel finds that this gesture of a rich and powerful man who, because of trials and tribulations of the times through which we are living, makes the gesture of renewing the bonds from which he had felt himself otherwise entirely freed, is a noble act which has made its deep impression on all of us. . . ."

The Baron puts down the newspaper.

BARON RAOUL: Well, if you want my opinion, it's not the nobility of his gesture that strikes me, but its utter stupidity! For a Jew to draw attention to his origins is the best way of making sure to arouse other people's animosity!

Borelli glances again at Alexandre, still looking for some reaction. But again Alexandre does not react, at least directly. He casts a quick eye back over at the lovely woman at the neighboring table. Then he turns back to Baron Raoul.

ALEXANDRE: Don't you ever read a Left Wing paper, Baron?

BARON RAOUL: Never, Sacha! I don't have the strength. They're too badly written!

As he continues to cast a flattering eye at the beautiful stranger across the lobby, Alexandre takes from the table a copy of another Right Wing paper, L'Action française, *and starts reading from it at random.*

ALEXANDRE: "The various presidents of State Councils and

Cabinet Ministers are for the most part blackguards, filthy no-good hooligans, and traitors who would best be served by taking a stick of dynamite and shoving it up their butts. . . ." Do you find that well written?

BARON RAOUL: But that's polemics, Sacha! We know that polemical writing is by definition excessive. . . . But you, Sacha, who are a man of taste, how can you hobnob with those Radical-Socialist members of Parliament?

Alexandre bursts out laughing.

ALEXANDRE: I don't hobnob with Radical-Socialists, Baron. I hobnob with power. Is it my fault if the Left coalition won the last elections?

Alexandre leans over close to the Baron, as if to tell him a secret.

ALEXANDRE: Let me make you a promise: if your friends win the next elections, we'll drink nothing but Taittinger champagne at my receptions!

The Baron smiles. So does the taciturn Borelli. As he is talking, Alexandre lifts his hand, and as if by magic a bellboy materializes. Alexandre takes out a visiting card (SERGE ALEXANDRE: Financial Advisor) and scribbles a few words on it. Then he gives some whispered instructions to the bellboy. At this point Borelli notices the young woman at the nearby table. The bellhop departs hurriedly.

BARON RAOUL (*voice over*): Why wait for the elections, Sacha? I can introduce you to my friends whenever you like. . . . You have nothing to lose. They may not hold the actual reins of power, but that doesn't mean they aren't powerful.

Again, Alexandre catches the eye of the young woman. Then he turns to Borelli:

ALEXANDRE: Albert, the checks are ready?

Borelli opens his briefcase and takes out some papers as well as several checkbooks. He gives the checks to Alexandre to sign, and even as he is signing them the latter gives his instructions:

ALEXANDRE: The first one I want you to cash yourself . . . fifty thousand francs for the Monetary and Development Fund . . . twenty-five thousand in an envelope for Véricourt. . . . Tell Laloy to take it over to him. . . . Bring the balance to me at the Empire.

On the check stub, Alexandre has made a note of how the total is to be divided. He tears off the check and hands it to Borelli, who then pushes another checkbook in his direction.

ALEXANDRE: Two hundred thousand! I want you to cash it at the C.I.C., then personally bring the money and deposit it at the Comédie-Française branch of the Crédit Lyonnais Bank. Of that total, transfer forty-five thousand to Biarritz and bring one hundred thousand francs over to the office and put it in the safe.

Borelli puts the papers and checkbooks neatly away in his briefcase.

Just as he does, the bellboy to whom Alexandre had given his calling card appears, carrying the card ostentatiously on a silver platter, while behind him six other bellhops file in laden with baskets of flowers which they set down in a semicircle at the feet of the astonished young woman. The first bellboy gives her Serge's calling card.

3.

The Office of the French Criminal Investigation Division in Paris—the Sûreté générale. The time is 10:30 a.m., July 24, 1933.

Inspector Boussaud is seen walking down a hallway in the Sûreté main building. Just as he approaches one of the doors that line the hallway it opens and a man whose name is Inspector Bonny appears. He is a thin, dapper, self-assured man.

BOUSSAUD: You leaving? I was just on my way to see you, Bonny!

Both men size each other up. Then Bonny makes a gesture which can be taken to mean: go on, speak your piece!

BOUSSAUD: Why are you so concerned about Alexandre?

Bonny feigns astonishment.

BONNY: Alexandre? Ah, yes, I'd forgotten that's how you refer to him. What makes you think I'm especially interested in him?

Boussaud shrugs his shoulders.

BOUSSAUD: Don't play dumb, Bonny! Since last May you've turned in three reports on Alexandre to the Investigative Services! Not to mention your newspaper campaign in *La Bonne Guerre*. Everyone knows how close you are to the paper's director. . . .

Bonny dryly interrupts Boussaud.

BONNY: Drop it, Boussaud! Do I go around worrying about your stoolies?

BOUSSAUD: The fact is, you worry far too much about mine!

Bonny's face suddenly lights up and he breaks into a short, ironic laugh.

BONNY: Oh, so that's it! Alexandre is still working for you!

BOUSSAUD: Listen to me, Bonny. . . . Put yourself in his shoes. How would you like it if people started digging around in your past? How would you feel if someone went and dug up, let's say the whole Vollberg case in your file at police head-quarters?

Bonny gives Boussaud a long, hard look. Then he smiles, a cynical smile.

BONNY: Having given the matter due thought, my dear colleague, I think it's best you and I sort this whole thing out right now!

He opens his office door, then stands aside holding the door to allow Boussaud to precede him into the office.

4.

The Hôtel Claridge in Paris. The time is 10:30 a.m., July 24, 1933.

In the hotel lobby, Alexandre has just gotten to his feet. The words he utters next are spoken loudly enough, no doubt, so that the young woman surrounded by bouquets of flowers can hear them.

ALEXANDRE: You see, my dear friend, you see how easy it is? That's all that money is. Little pieces of paper that Borelli handles for us!

Borelli and the Baron get to their feet, and Alexandre leads them toward the exit, still managing to glance at the young woman to see what her reaction is.

ALEXANDRE: Let's be off, Baron. They're waiting for us at the Empire!

As he walks he manages to turn and, obviously pleased with his quip, says in the general direction of the young woman:

ALEXANDRE: At Alexandre's Empire!

It is clear that she has been mesmerized by the man.

5.

The Hôtel Claridge, then at the Théâtre de l'Empire in Paris. Between 10:30 and 11:00 a.m., July 24, 1933.

In front of the Claridge, Baron Raoul and Alexandre wait for the latter's limousine to arrive. Borelli has already left.

ALEXANDRE: I want to know everything, Baron! Down to the last little detail, so that I can imagine I was really there to witness Arlette's triumph!

BARON RAOUL: It was more than a triumph, Sacha, it was a veritable apotheosis! Everything contributed to it. . . . The weather was perfect. . . .

As Alexandre's Rolls Royce pulls up in front of the Claridge, we see a whole other set of images.

*

Baron Raoul arrives at the main entrance of the Hôtel du Palais in Biarritz. Again we see the elegant little crowd. In the background, the ocean.

BARON RAOUL (*voice over*): . . . the hydrangeas were in full bloom, that azure blue you love as much as I do. . . . The sea, but a stone's throw away, with its emerald waves and white foam mingling with the blue of the flowers . . .

As he speaks, we see the Baron in an elevator rising toward the upper stories of the hotel.

In the hallway of one of the upper floors the Baron knocks gently on the door to one of the suites. Then he goes in.

We view the scene from outside the hotel, that is, follow the progress of Baron Raoul—or at least of his silhouette—as he makes his way through the various rooms of Arlette's suite. As he walks, the Baron meets a maid carrying a dress over her arm. The camera picks up that maid and follows her as she walks through another room, where she meets and passes a second maid who is carrying a hat.

In the last room of the suite we finally come upon—still viewed from the outside, that is, the balcony of the hotel (respects to Lubitsch, an intentional theft from Trouble in Paradise*!)—Arlette, in a state of partial undress, trying on different dresses.*

*

We're back again in the Rolls Royce which is taking Baron Raoul and Alexandre to the Théâtre de l'Empire.

ALEXANDRE: A bad dream? What bad dream?

BARON RAOUL: She dreamed that you were both falling, together—dreams of falling are commonplace, Sacha!—in a car whose brakes didn't work!

ALEXANDRE: That's odd. That's been a recurring dream with Arlette recently. I must remember to talk to Mézy about it!

Baron Raoul shrugs his shoulders.

ALEXANDRE: Is Montalvo still running after my wife?

BARON RAOUL: Nothing, but nothing deters our Don Juan! Again yesterday he turned his Hispano-Suiza over to Arlette for whatever needs she might have.

    *

As Baron Raoul utters these words we return to the scene of the luxury-car competition in front of the Hôtel du Palais in Biarritz.
  Montalvo accompanies Arlette to a gleaming Hispano-Suiza. Montalvo himself is at the wheel as the car drives up to the

spot where the jury—which includes the Baron Raoul—is seated. The car stops, and Montalvo opens the door for Arlette, who rewards him with a radiant yet distant smile. She takes a few steps along the car and then assumes the traditional pose leaning back up against the car.

*

At the end of that remembered scene, punctuated by music, we are in front of the Théâtre de l'Empire in Paris.

A poster announces that the theater is closed for rehearsals,

16

but we can also see the posters for the previous show: KATINKA, in huge letters.

Alexandre and Baron Raoul go into the theater through the stage door. As they walk through the corridors of the theater, Alexandre says:

ALEXANDRE: What ever happened to Montalvo's well-laid plans? Is he still conspiring to overthrow the Republic in Spain?

BARON RAOUL: I haven't the faintest notion, Sacha! All I know is that he is currently making plans to go to Italy. . . .

Alexandre stops in his tracks. He is thinking out loud.

ALEXANDRE: Italy? That means they're making contact with Mussolini. Of course! That's it. Mussolini!

6.

The Théâtre de l'Empire in Paris. 11:00 a.m., July 24, 1933.

Alexandre and the Baron go into the administrative offices of the theater.

On the walls we see posters of Katinka, and a number of photographs. In a vase on a table is a magnificent bouquet of bright red carnations.

Someone gets up to greet them as they come in: Dr. Mézy, a man of about fifty.

ALEXANDRE: Morning, Doc.

Alexandre goes directly to the bouquet of carnations. He chooses one and, removing the one he had been wearing, places the fresh one in his buttonhole.

Dr. Mézy's words are addressed to the Baron. He speaks in a precise, authoritarian way.

DR. MÉZY: If you'll kindly excuse me, my friend, I'm going to need a few minutes of Alexandre's time. I have to examine him!

The Baron is clearly surprised. As for Alexandre, he is embarrassed. One has the feeling that he doesn't exactly enjoy

having his health discussed in front of other people. But the
doctor seems to be making a point of the matter, almost as
though he were trying to establish a dominant position vis-à-vis
Alexandre, and goes on:

DR. MÉZY: He worries too much! Has insomnia and sieges of
depression. And that doesn't please me one little bit!

With considerable authority he leads Alexandre away with him
into a neighboring room, leaving the Baron alone.
Baron Raoul begins pacing to and fro across the room,
mechanically looking at the posters and photographs.

BARON RAOUL: Should I have told Sacha?

He takes a few more steps, then pauses in front of a photo of a
young blond actress whose name, according to the caption un-
derneath, is RITA GEORG.

18

BARON RAOUL: Not to say anything to him is a kind of betrayal. But to mention it to him would hardly be gallant. . . .

*

With these words, the images passing through the Baron's mind suddenly appear on the screen.

Arlette and Juan Montalvo are shown in a lush green setting, which turns out to be the Chiberta golf course in Biarritz. Both are dressed in golf outfits of the period.

We see the pair as through a pair of binoculars, which is precisely how they are being viewed by the Baron, who is seated on the shaded terrace of the golf club.

BARON RAOUL (*voice over*): Yesterday, after Arlette's triumph, Montalvo made up his mind to make a final assault in an effort to overcome the lady's resistance. "Double or nothing" was the way he put it to me. "Either that woman will be mine tonight or I'll disappear!"

The Baron is watching them through his binoculars. We can see them both clearly, but because we can't hear them, just what is going on remains unclear.

Instead of stepping up to the ball and hitting it, Arlette is standing next to Montalvo, listening to him.

Baron Raoul lowers his binoculars.

BARON RAOUL (*voice over*): What is she saying to him? Arlette looks absolutely entranced.

In the distance where they are standing, Arlette finally moves over to the golf ball and hits it. Then she and Juan start walking in the direction the ball has taken down the fairway.

   Montalvo has taken Arlette by the arm. But after they have taken only a few steps, they stop again. They are facing each other, talking. At one point, Arlette reaches up and puts her hand on Montalvo's shoulder. He takes her hand and kisses it.

   When next we hear the Baron's voice, it is terribly excited and upset.

BARON RAOUL (*voice over*): But what are they talking about? They both look terribly upset!

     *

Suddenly we find ourselves right next to Arlette and Montalvo—there is no longer any need for the binoculars. As they stand in this idyllic, peaceful setting of Chiberta, Arlette is listening, as though mesmerized, to a strange story.

MONTALVO: Thirty thousand acres of land that my ancestors won back by force from the Arabs, acres of vineyards and olive orchards that are rightfully mine, that have come down to me through the centuries from my family. So I raised my hand and the lieutenant of the *Guardia Civil* gave the order to shoot!

He gives a brief, almost abortive laugh.

MONTALVO: . . . In Spain, the peasants are shot at point-blank range. We and death are old, old friends!

With a graceful movement, Arlette takes her stroke. Then Montalvo takes her arm again as they stroll down the fairway.

MONTALVO: Why is it you persist in arranging it so you're never alone with me? Are you afraid you might weaken?

There is a great deal of male conceit in his tone. Arlette turns and faces him with a smile.

ARLETTE: I fear nothing of the sort, my dear Juan. I am not a virtuous woman. Nor do I respect the sacrament of marriage.

Montalvo is completely taken aback. What is she driving at?

ARLETTE: But I belong to a man, literally. He alone can free me from that condition of servitude. And do you know what? The only thing in the world that I am afraid of is that he might do it!

They stand there looking at each other for a long moment. She puts her hand on his shoulder; he takes it and kisses it.

7.

The Théâtre de l'Empire in Paris. 11:45 a.m., July 24, 1933.

Two other characters have now joined the Baron, Alexandre, and Dr. Mézy in the administrative offices of the theater. One of them is Gaston Henriet, a fat, rather vulgar man, who is Alexandre's friend and associate. His interests are horseracing, jewels, and the theater. The other person is Monsieur Grammont, a young, brilliant, and ambitious lawyer.

Alexandre is talking to Henriet.

ALEXANDRE: . . . What about putting on A *Penny's Worth of Flowers* in a more modest way? I don't know . . . maybe we could use the same sets as for *Katinka*.

HENRIET: Come on, Alex, the public wants something new and fresh. That's what it always wants!

Baron Raoul interrupts.

BARON RAOUL: Gaston's got a point, Sacha! When people find it hard to make it to the end of the month without pinching and scraping, they go to the theater to get their mind onto something else. They want to see luxury, dancing, something bright and shiny. Everything they don't have. They want to be persuaded that life is easy!

HENRIET: On that score you have no quarrel, right Alex? Life *is* easy.

Alexandre shrugs his shoulders in resignation.

ALEXANDRE: If the Baron agrees with you, I have no choice but to give up. Go ahead with A *Penny's Worth of Flowers*.

He turns to the young lawyer.

ALEXANDRE: You'll see, my friend, how many millions of francs that "Penny" is going to cost me!

They all laugh. Alexandre takes out a pocket watch.

ALEXANDRE: Gentlemen, it's time for the auditions. Start them without me. Monsieur Grammont and I have a little business to transact.

Then, addressing himself to Dr. Mézy:

ALEXANDRE: Don't go away! I need you too!

8.

The Sûreté générale *in Paris. Twelve noon, July 24, 1933.*

Inspector Boussaud is leaving Inspector Bonny's office. Bonny has accompanied him to the door and is standing on the threshold. Seated on a bench in the hallway, a man is waiting. Bonny signals to him. As Inspector Boussaud leaves, he glances over at the seated man.

BONNY: I'm sorry I kept you waiting. . . .

In Bonny's office the man has spread a file on Bonny's table. From it he takes Le Petit Journal illustré—*an illustrated weekly scandal sheet of the day—whose gaudy cover depicts the arrest of the rogue and swindler Stavisky on a night in July 1926 at Marly-le-Roi, outside of Paris.*

BLACKMAILER: This is what I've dreamed up for Alexandre. . . . This illustration is going to appear in our next issue, with the caption: "The owner of the newspaper *La Volonté*, and of the Empire Theater, in the course of a little surprise party. . . ." How does that strike you, Bonny?

Bonny looks at the cover of Le Petit Journal illustré. *Then he shakes his head.*

BONNY: I've changed my mind. . . . Alexandre is on his guard.

The blackmailer's expression is one of intense curiosity, but he knows that he shouldn't become too involved in the whole affair.

BLACKMAILER: In that case, what do you want me to do?

BONNY: Go and see him anyway.

He opens a drawer and takes out a piece of paper, which he hands to the other man.

BONNY: What I'm giving you is a little item I picked up from Biarritz. . . . Turn it into something more innocuous. . . . Just to prime the pump. . . . I like the idea that you're in direct contact with him.

The blackmailer looks down and reads the item which Bonny has just handed him.

9.

The Théâtre de l'Empire in Paris. The time is 12:15 p.m., July 24, 1933.

Dr. Mézy is holding in his hand a copy of the scandal sheet newspaper La Bonne Guerre. *All we can see is part of the headline: ". . . alias Serge Alexandre. Is he an Untouchable?" And below it the subhead: ". . . because he's the director of a major paper and the head of the Théâtre de l'Empire, he spends money hand over fist at the Hôtel Claridge and elsewhere."*

Alexandre, who is standing, takes the paper from Dr. Mézy's hands and starts pacing the floor.

ALEXANDRE: It's not this two-bit paper that bothers me. I've had a long relationship with such scandal sheets. . . .

We see Monsieur Grammont, who is seated at the desk, on which he has set up his files.

ALEXANDRE: It's who is behind that paper that bothers me: Inspector Bonny. He turned in a report on me on May twenty-third, another on June seventeenth, and the latest one as recently as July first. Less than a month ago!

Alexandre goes over and hands the newspaper back to Grammont, who puts it in one of his files.

GRAMMONT: You're well informed!

ALEXANDRE: I ought to be, for what I pay! My contributions to the police health fund cost me more than a mad mistress would!

They all laugh. Alexandre goes on:

ALEXANDRE: Grammont, we have to get to the root of the problem. . . . And the root is the Laforcade file. . . .

Grammont is about to speak, but Alexandre doesn't let him.

ALEXANDRE: I want one thing to be crystal clear, Grammont. I want to get this thing over with, once and for all. . . . The

trial's been hanging fire for seven years. . . . I've finagled a
dozen postponements, which is not to be sneezed at. But
I want a final "not guilty"; I want all the plaintiffs involved
to drop their charges. Or invoke the statute of limitations. . . .
We have enough friends on the bench and in the ministries
to find a solution!

GRAMMONT: The fact is . . . I have spoken about it to Véricourt. . . . We have a plan. . . . We'll have to pay off the
plaintiffs in order to get them to drop their charges. . . .
With two million francs I know I can bring it off. But now
that I know the file, I want to ask you a few questions. . . .

Alexandre makes a gesture to interrupt him.

ALEXANDRE: You can ask any questions you like. But not to me.

To Dr. Mézy. That's why I asked him to come here today. As for me, I've forgotten. I made up my mind to forget.

His tone changes.

ALEXANDRE: I'm Serge Alexandre, financial advisor, director of a major theater, owner of a string of racehorses, silent partner in several newspapers. This fall, I'm finalizing plans to set up my International Monetary and Development Fund, with five hundred million francs' worth of shares outstanding. Quoted on the stock exchange, and guaranteed by the State! So you can understand why I don't want to hear any more about that poor jerk out on parole, those second-rate deals! That person, Grammont, has got to disappear from my life!

Saying this, Alexandre stalks out of the office.

10.

The Théâtre de l'Empire. The time is 12:30 p.m., July 24, 1933.

The doctor and lawyer remain behind alone in the office.

DR. MÉZY: There, you've seen it for yourself. The man is totally sincere: a typical case of schizophrenia. The person he once was has become someone else: a ghost he despises. But a ghost who worries him.

Grammont has taken from the file a copy of Le Petit Journal illustré *whose cover depicts the arrest of Stavisky at Marly-le-Roi on July 26, 1926.*

GRAMMONT: Well, I can tell you that the arrest in July of twenty-six was no dream.

Dr. Mézy comes over to the desk and looks at the gaudy drawing on the cover of Le Petit Journal illustré.

DR. MÉZY: Not exactly a realistic portrayal, is it? In fact, it was a rather ordinary police raid. . . .

As Dr. Mézy continues his recital of the facts of that fateful day, we see the scenes that his reminiscences evoke. It is early

evening on a summer's day. Police cars surround a suburban house in the town of Marly-le-Roi, a rather isolated house set amidst a cluster of shade trees. Plainclothesmen emerge from the cars.

DR. MÉZY *(voice over)*: Alex had been in hiding for three months. There was a warrant out for his arrest. Fraud, receipt and concealment of stolen goods, checks written without funds to cover them.

The police begin to infiltrate the yard surrounding the house, behind which they note a powerful car, on whose roof baggage has already been strapped.
The police are merely darker shadows in the already shadowy yard; they approach the bay windows of the room in the house which is brightly lighted.

DR. MÉZY *(voice over)*: Alex had been forewarned. He has always had his personal contacts in the police force.

A ray of light hits one of the policemen who, guns in hand, invade the house itself: it is Inspector Boussaud.

28

DR. MÉZY *(voice over)*: He had plenty of time to make a clean getaway. But no, he insisted on throwing a farewell dinner for his friends. . . . Alex loves parties. . . .

Peering through the bay window, Inspector Boussaud sees a brightly lit room. A dining room, set for eleven guests. Immaculate table linen, flowers everywhere, ice buckets for the champagne. Among those present we recognize Borelli, Gaston Henriet, Dr. Mézy, Arlette.

Inspector Boussaud raises his arm, and from all sides the policemen swarm into the villa. Arlette starts to her feet. Glass is breaking, the flowers are overturned.

The guests are herded together in the dining room. Boussaud is there, directing operations. Two other inspectors arrive with Alexandre between them. He is furious. Alexandre and Boussaud exchange long, hard looks.

*

We move in on Boussaud's face, until he is framed in a close-up in such a way as to isolate him from the set of the Marly-le-Roi dining room. The soundtrack also changes. We hear the rustling

of papers, an occasional cough: the sounds one hears in a room where a certain number of people meet to listen to someone speak.

The person speaking is Boussaud. To whom is he speaking? We will not find out until later. For the moment, the impression given is rather disturbing.

BOUSSAUD: I arrested him at Marly-le-Roi. Two years later I ran into him in a café. He was out of prison. He said the charges against him had finally been dropped. He agreed to become an informer for me, and ultimately furnished me with a number of interesting pieces of information having to do with swindlers, counterfeiters, and drunks. It was a world he knew firsthand.

*

Again we are back in the administrative offices of the Théâtre de l'Empire. Monsieur Grammont is just putting back into its file the cover of Le Petit Journal illustré *depicting Stavisky's arrest.*

We hear Dr. Mézy's voice as he goes on with his story:

DR. MÉZY (*voice over*): The day after his son's arrest, Alex's father, a decent, hard-working dentist who lived in a respectable section of Paris, shot himself in the head.

Dr. Mézy appears. He moves away from the desk and goes over to an easy chair on the other side of the office and sits down.

DR. MÉZY: And then there's the matter of women. . . .

Grammont indicates that he is in total agreement and takes a document from his file.

GRAMMONT: I have here a police report dated April 1926. "He has no clearly defined means of existence. . . . Lazy, and of dubious moral character, he appears to depend for his funds on exploiting women, with whom he has considerable success. . . ."

DR. MÉZY: There's one episode that strikes me as of prime importance. You won't find it in that file. . . . In order to understand Alex, you sometimes have to forget the files. You have to dream about him, try and imagine what his dreams are. . . .

        *

A series of images flash on the screen: colonnades near the fountains of the Parc Monceau in Paris. The façades of the Condorcet Lycée. Other façades typical of Paris in the early years of the century. And then another shot of the Parc Monceau, with the stone pyramid half hidden among the greenery.

Over these shots, Dr. Mézy's voice continues to be heard.

DR. MÉZY (*voice over*): Alex was sixteen. Still a student at the Condorcet Lycée in Paris. A woman of about thirty, apparently of slightly dubious reputation, was quite smitten by him. . . .

Now we follow through the corridors of some deserted palace the evanescent image of a woman dressed in white.

DR. MÉZY *(voice over)*: . . . She kidnapped him as it were and spirited him off to Deauville with her, where she initiated him into the secrets of life. . . . Alex saw, for the first time in his life, a whole new universe of wealth, pleasure, gambling. . . . It was, you might say, a turning point. . . .

Dr. Mézy's "voice over" is suddenly interrupted by Alex's voice, also heard "voice over."

ALEXANDRE *(voice over)*: You have it all wrong, Doc . . .

Alexandre has just stepped back into the office at the Empire, his face wreathed in a broad smile.

ALEXANDRE: . . . all wrong! It wasn't that woman who initiated me into the realities of life. It was my own grandfather!

The two other men look at him with interest.

ALEXANDRE: He was great! As great in fact as my father was solemn, afraid of his own shadow, and imbued with the notion of respectability. My grandfather was a whole other cup of tea! When I was a singer, doing my act at the Wagram Concerts, he came to see me perform every single night! . . . He taught me everything I know!

From the doorway, Alexandre is still smiling broadly as he looks at both men.

ALEXANDRE: I wanted to tell you to come and join us when you've finished. These auditions are great fun.

And on these words he exits.

1

The Théâtre de l'Empire. The time is 12:45 p.m., July 24, 1933.

Alexandre is walking down the long center aisle of the orchestra of the Théâtre de l'Empire. He takes a seat in one of the first

rows, next to Gaston Henriet and Baron Raoul.

The young actresses summoned for the audition are seated in various places throughout the orchestra. The stage manager, who is seated on the stage itself, calls out a name:

STAGE MANAGER: Mademoiselle Zambeaux!

No one moves. Apparently the actress called is not there. He goes on to the next name on the list.

STAGE MANAGER: Mademoiselle Édith Boréal!

Édith Boréal is a comely blond woman with a lively and grace-ful air. She climbs up onto the stage carrying a play pamphlet in her hand. She emanates a feeling of self-assurance.

The sets for Katinka have never been struck, so she will be auditioning with, as background, a snow-covered Russian Ortho-dox church.

HENRIET: What are you going to audition?

ÉDITH BOREAL: Sacha Guitry's *I Love You*. Act 5, the scene

between "him" and "her."

STAGE MANAGER: And where is "him"?

ÉDITH BORÉAL: He stood me up at the last minute. Would you mind reading his part for me?

STAGE MANAGER: You think that's part of my job?

In the orchestra, Baron Raoul has been following their exchange. He gets to his feet.

BARON RAOUL: If Mademoiselle has a copy of the play with her I'd be happy to give it a try!

ALEXANDRE: An excellent idea, Baron!

Baron Raoul clambers up the wooden walkway by which one proceeds from the orchestra to the stage.
As he does, Borelli appears in the background and walks down the aisle until he reaches the row where Alexandre is sitting. He leans over and whispers something in his ear.
Alexandre gets up, but still keeps his eyes on the action on stage.
Baron Raoul goes over to the young actress and greets her courteously.
Édith Boréal shows him her copy of the play and explains to him what he's supposed to do.
Still watching what is happening on stage, Alexandre, accompanied by Borelli, retreats back up the aisle toward the orchestra lobby. Baron Raoul and Édith Boréal have begun their scene.

BARON RAOUL/HE: "I've done it! I've actually managed to pull it off! You have a house of your own!"

ÉDITH BORÉAL/SHE: "Can I look at the bedroom?"

BARON RAOUL/HE: "Go right ahead. It's your bedroom. But come back . . . or call me to join you."

ÉDITH BORÉAL/SHE: "Oh, I can't believe it!"

BARON RAOUL/HE: "What can't you believe?"

ÉDITH BORÉAL/SHE: "The bedroom! It has everything! Closets . . . linen, everything for the dressing table! . . . Oh, can I peek into the dining room?"

BARON RAOUL/HE: "Please do. . . . It's your house to visit."

Édith Boréal dashes to and fro on stage, pretending to visit every room in the house.

ÉDITH BORÉAL/SHE: "Oh, how beautiful it is. Oh, what a lovely table cloth! . . . And the butler's tray . . . and the glasses! And the plates . . . it's all so stunning! Oh! I forgot to look at the bathroom!"

And she dashes back across stage.

BARON RAOUL/HE: "Is there a bathtub?"

ÉDITH BORÉAL/SHE: "Oh! It's unbelievable. . . . Goodness, I forgot to see whether there were any knives!"

And again she dashes across the stage.

35

BARON RAOUL/HE: "Don't touch the knives, for goodness' sake. You might cut yourself!"

ÉDITH BORÉAL/SHE: "Oh, I forgot to check the linen closet."

At this point in their scene, we see that Alexandre and Borelli have reached the back of the orchestra. They exit into the lobby.

*

Walking in step, Alexandre and Borelli silently make their way through the labyrinthine corridors of the theater toward the actors' dressing rooms.

Without a word Borelli hands Alexandre an envelope. He opens it, takes out a fat wad of banknotes, and stuffs them in his pocket. He crumples up the envelope and tosses it away.

Alexandre and Borelli go into one of the actors' dressing rooms. The Blackmailer, whom we have seen earlier in Inspector Bonny's office, is seated there. As they enter, he gets to his feet.

Alexandre looks at him but says nothing. He takes his watch from his watch pocket.

ALEXANDRE: I'll give you five minutes!

The man's smile is simultaneously insolent and obsequious. He takes a piece of paper from his pocket and hands it to Alexandre.

BLACKMAILER: This item will appear in our next issue of the paper, which will be on the stands next week. I thought it might interest you, Monsieur Alexandre.

The man lays a heavy stress on the name "Alexandre." But the latter refuses his piece of paper with a peremptory gesture of his hand.

ALEXANDRE: I presume it was you who wrote it. Therefore read it yourself!

For a brief moment the Blackmailer seems to lose his composure. Then he gets hold of himself, smiles, and reads the bit of gossip.

BLACKMAILER: "Biarritz. A few days ago the gaming tables of this city witnessed what by any standards have to be considered huge stakes: two hundred to three hundred thousand francs were bet by a number of baccarat professionals: Henriet, Garcia, Serge Alexandre . . ."

The Blackmailer breaks off for a moment to glance up and see what Alexandre's reaction is. But the subject of his gossip gives him no satisfaction, so he resumes reading:

BLACKMAILER: ". . . Alexandre . . . the Strovosky of the phony Hungarian securities . . ."

Again the Blackmailer breaks off, this time to comment on what he has just read.

BLACKMAILER: I hope you'll excuse the misspelling. But our typesetters have trouble with all these foreign names!

He prepares to resume reading, but Alexandre stops him, again with a gesture of his hand.

ALEXANDRE: That's enough! Casino gossip leaves me cold: I'm completely covered in that area. Your friends in the vice squad should have cued you in!

He smiles, then laughs derisively. The Blackmailer smiles too, almost automatically.

ALEXANDRE: As for the Hungarian securities, they're good as gold!

He turns to Borelli.

ALEXANDRE: Send this gentleman the full documentation on the Hungarian securities and the International Monetary and Development Fund. Yes, and the text drawn up after consulting with Monsieur Vannier of the State Banking Commission.

Again he flashes a broad smile at the Blackmailer.

ALEXANDRE: No, my friend, your silly little piece of idle gossip leaves me absolutely cold!

The Blackmailer bows ever so slightly, puts his piece of paper back in his pocket. But Alexandre hasn't finished yet.

ALEXANDRE: But there is something else that does interest me, and that's your little newspaper! Two months ago I founded a company known as S.A.P.E.P., the head of which is my friend here, Borelli. . . .

He gestures toward Borelli, who is standing behind him.

ALEXANDRE: The purpose of the company is to group a certain number of magazines and newspapers for advertising purposes. . . . Several are already signed up: *Cyrano, Le Cri du jour, Le Carnet de la semaine, Bec et ongles* . . . and we're negotiating with two others.

BLACKMAILER: And what about my paper? I might be interested in working out some kind of deal with you.

ALEXANDRE: With your paper, my friend, it's not a question of a deal. With you it's a misdeal!

The Blackmailer shakes his head, but Alexandre goes on before he can say anything further.

ALEXANDRE: But since you're interested, Borelli can give you all the details about it.

He takes out his watch, glances at it, makes a gesture which indicates that his time has run out, and heads for the door. On the threshold he turns and says to Borelli:

ALEXANDRE: You can give the gentleman something on account.

He exits. Borelli, as ordered, goes over and starts peeling off banknotes, which he hands to the Blackmailer.

*

Alexandre reappears in the auditorium of the Théâtre de l'Empire. But instead of taking his former place in the orchestra, he sits down in a loge seat overlooking the stage.

Baron Raoul and Édith Boréal are just winding up their reading.

BARON RAOUL/HE: "I want our love to be simple, uncomplicated, like the accounts of happy people in history books. . . . I want those not privy to our love to be completely baffled by it. How can I put it? . . . Let's say that if one day a dramatist were to have the ridiculous idea of writing a play about us, about our love . . . the critics would be compelled to say: 'But that's not a play. . . . Nothing ever happens!' "

Baron Raoul and Édith Boréal both leave the stage. The Stage Manager calls out the name of another candidate.

STAGE MANAGER: Erna Wolfgang!

At some point earlier we will have noticed Erna Wolfgang among those seated in the auditorium, for the simple reason that there is something rather special about her.

Before the Stage Manager has a chance to ask her any questions, she advances toward the footlights.

ERNA WOLFGANG: I can sing, dance, and act. I am also an acrobat and have experience on the high wire. But as you may have noticed I speak with an accent.

She smiles and takes a deep breath, in preparation for what is to follow. But what she has said has already had an effect on her audience, who are listening to her intently now. The Stage Manager is watching her with certain misgivings. Alexandre has leaned forward in his box overlooking the stage, his elbows on the railing.

ERNA WOLFGANG: I'm Jewish. I've just arrived from Berlin.

It is so silent you can hear a pin drop, but it is a very special silence: one of attentiveness. Even the Stage Manager has succumbed to her spell. Alexandre, Baron Raoul, and Henriet are all staring at her, as are Dr. Mézy and the lawyer Grammont, who by now have arrived in the auditorium.
  Erna, looking out over the almost empty theater, goes on:

ERNA WOLFGANG: Since the Germans seized power earlier this
  year it is harder and harder for us to live in Germany.

She pauses for a moment, and smiles.

ERNA WOLFGANG: Not that it has ever been easy for us to live
  anywhere in the world!

With this brief background, she goes on with specifics.

ERNA WOLFGANG: The last play I performed in Germany was
  called *Die Massnahme.* . . . But the theater was closed down
  by the police. . . . So, here I am!

She smiles again. But no one stirs; the silence is leaden. Obviously, those most impressed by her words are Alexandre and the Stage Manager.

ERNA WOLFGANG: I had prepared a monologue, but after seeing
  what this kind gentleman just did (*turning toward Baron
  Raoul*), I thought perhaps you might want to read with me,
  too.

Baron Raoul is both flattered and embarrassed. He makes a gesture which expresses what he feels, as Erna goes on.

ERNA WOLFGANG: If it doesn't strike you as too insulting to the genius and spirit of France, I would like to play for you a scene from Giraudoux's *Intermezzo*. But for that I need a ghost!

She is still talking to Baron Raoul. One has the feeling he is ready and willing to oblige her and play the part of the Ghost. Despite his preconceived ideas about the Jewish question, this flesh-and-blood Jew has apparently charmed him.

But before Baron Raoul has a chance to reply, we hear Alexandre's voice from the box above.

ALEXANDRE *(voice over)*: Allow me, Baron!

All eyes turn up toward Alexandre, including Erna's.

ALEXANDRE: The part of a ghost may just be tailor-made for me!

The Stage Manager turns to Erna and nods, implying that she ought to accept his offer.

ERNA WOLFGANG: All right, come on down. I have a script you can read from.

In her hand she is holding a copy of the magazine La Petite Illustration *which contains the Giraudoux play.*

Alexandre goes up onto the stage and is now standing next to Erna.

ERNA WOLFGANG *(pointing to the script)*: I've made some cuts, see? Here's where my scene begins.

ALEXANDRE: What am I supposed to do?

Erna pulls up a small bench and moves Alexandre in back of it.

ERNA WOLFGANG: You float there behind me.

From his seat in the orchestra, Henriet pipes up and, in a jovial mood, says:

HENRIET: Just read your part, Alex! And try to put yourself in the proper frame of mind!

ERNA WOLFGANG: I'm seated on a bench. It's nighttime. . . . Monsieur, can we have a little night, please?

HENRIET: Let there be night!

Just then, Borelli enters the auditorium through the doors in the back and stops in his tracks, obviously not believing his eyes.

The stage is now darkened, simulating night. One projector stabs through the darkness and focuses on Erna and Alexandre. Erna is now seated on the bench, with Alexandre stationed behind, holding a copy of La Petite Illustration *in his hand. He begins to read.*

ALEXANDRE/GHOST: "No . . . All the dead are extraordinarily clever. . . ."

Alexandre stops in mid-speech, probably somewhat taken aback by the lines he has just read. Erna turns to him and signals for him to go on.

ALEXANDRE/GHOST: "No. All the dead are extraordinarily clever. . . . They never stumble against the void. They never get caught on any shadows. . . . They never trip over nothingness. . . . And nothing ever illuminates their faces."

Shot of Borelli, still standing in the center aisle of the orchestra.

*

Suddenly, we see a close-up of Borelli's face, isolated from the setting of the Théâtre de l'Empire. The soundtrack is also different. Again we hear, as we did for Inspector Boussaud, the rustling of papers and the coughing of people whom we can't see. Borelli speaks slowly, as though weighing every word.

BORELLI: The simplest answer is this: he was crazy. . . . Isn't it obvious, Mister Chairman, that when a man has just got out of prison his primary concern is to make sure people forget him. . . .

    *

Return to Borelli at the Théâtre de l'Empire. And to Erna Wolfgang's voice reading from Intermezzo:

ERNA WOLFGANG/ISABELLE *(voice over):* ". . . which makes them like their condition and understand that they're immortal?"

We are back on stage. Alexandre is reading his part.

ALEXANDRE/GHOST: "They aren't."

ERNA WOLFGANG/ISABELLE: "What do you mean?"

ALEXANDRE/GHOST: "They die too!"

ERNA WOLFGANG/ISABELLE: "Isn't it odd how little the different races know about one another. American Indians think they're red, blacks think they're white, the dead think they're mortal!"

The scene is over. Alexandre and Erna are standing looking at each other.

12.

Southern France. The time is 1:30 p.m., July 24, 1933.

Shot of the automobile carrying Trotsky and his wife as it drives at a good clip down a southern country road bordered by plane trees, followed by the second car, bearing Inspector Gardet.

13.

The Théâtre de l'Empire. The time is 1:35 p.m., July 24, 1933.

Erna Wolfgang and Alexandre are walking through the corridors of the Empire Theatre, toward the actors' entrance.

ALEXANDRE: Why do you make such a point of telling the whole world you're Jewish?

Erna looks at him.

ERNA WOLFGANG: Because it's true.

ALEXANDRE: That, if I may say so, Mademoiselle, is a reply as simple as it is silly!

She laughs and shakes her head.

ERNA WOLFGANG: You want a more intelligent answer, something more "theatrical"?

He nods. She stops and begins to assume a theatrical tone, as though what she were saying were a memorized text.

ERNA WOLFGANG: Because when I wake up in the morning and look at the trees, at the dew on the grass, at the blue that dreams are made of, I know that I'm Jewish. Because I loathe races that don't know who they are and what they are. I loathe the Jewish race for believing it is happy and content and equal before the law, forgetting all the disasters through which it has lived!

He looks at her.

ALEXANDRE: And where does that get you?

ERNA WOLFGANG: It allows me to be myself. That is, different.

He smiles, but there is something strange about it.

ALEXANDRE: You know what my father always used to say?

ERNA WOLFGANG: I can guess.

ALEXANDRE: Make sure not to stand out, Sacha, he would say. Don't be first in your class, it will only make the others jealous. Don't be last, either, because then they'll look down on you. Somewhere in the middle, Sacha, where no one will notice you. That way, people will leave you alone.

ERNA WOLFGANG: But it doesn't work, does it? They don't leave us alone. . . . Where are you from?

ALEXANDRE: Russia. (*Then, with almost no transition:*) I'd give a lot to make sure you have a happy life.

She laughs and shakes her head. Alexandre takes, with a gesture we now know is part of his makeup, his watch from his pocket.

ALEXANDRE: Thirty seconds . . . Thirty seconds before you reach the street. Thirty seconds in which to offer you happiness. That's not much time. Let's not even discuss pleasure. For pleasure, a whole lifetime is hardly enough!

Erna laughs. Obviously, she enjoys the company of this man whom she has never met.

ERNA WOLFGANG: I always heard the opposite was true.

ALEXANDRE: People say a lot of inanities on the subject. But happiness is a question of the moment: the reflection of sun on the water. In the best instances, a succession of moments. But pleasure is something else altogether: it requires reflection. . . . You need time, plenty of free time, and a fair amount of wit: pleasure is the province of the wealthy!

Again she laughs, intrigued by Alexandre.

ERNA WOLFGANG: What's your position here? What do you do?

ALEXANDRE: Everything. I own the whole place. It is, you might say, my Empire!

They both laugh.

ALEXANDRE: I can offer you Paris.

ERNA WOLFGANG: Thanks. But I don't want it. I prefer happiness.

46

They've arrived at the end of the corridor leading to the stage door. Erna gives him one last look, turns, opens the door, and disappears. A splash of sunlight as she goes.

14.

The South of France. The time is 1:45 p.m., July 24, 1933.

A shady terrace of a country inn, situated close beside a stream.
   At a table in the foreground, we see Inspector Gardet. Seated at another table in the shade we can see, from Inspector Gardet's point of view, the white silhouette of Trotsky, his wife, and friends.

15.

The Hôtel Claridge in Paris. The time is 6:30 p.m., July 24, 1933.

A room in the Claridge. In a rumpled bed, half hidden in the sheets, lies the pretty young woman to whom Alexandre had *sent a mountain of flowers that morning.*

Seated on the edge of the bed, Alexandre is getting dressed. When he slips on his suitcoat and is ready to leave, he notes that his carnation is no longer fresh; he plucks it from his button-hole and tosses it away.

YOUNG WOMAN: You flustered me, you know. I hope I didn't cry out too loud?

Alexandre's smile in lieu of a reply is a bit mechanical. He makes a gesture indicating "good-bye" and leaves the room.

He takes a few steps down the hotel hallway, until he reaches a point a few yards away where Borelli has been sitting waiting, killing time by reading a sports magazine.

As Alexandre goes by, Borelli quickly gets up, sticks his magazine in his pocket, and follows his boss. Both men walk along without speaking.

We next see them in the elevator taking them up to Alexandre's suite on a higher floor. Borelli is looking at Alexandre, with a questioning eye.

Without any preamble, Alexandre starts declaiming:

ALEXANDRE: "The dear lady lay unclothed,
              Knowing my heart on fire,
              Clad only in her royal jewels
              A strange yet comely attire,
              A garb of such resplendent lure
              As draped the lovely fools
              Of yore: those happy slaves of Moors. . . ."

Only a slight movement of his eye belies Borelli's apparent self-control, but the elevator boy cannot refrain from casting an admiring glance in Alexandre's direction.

The elevator door opens, and Alexandre and Borelli emerge. The elevator boy literally gapes at them as they disappear down the hallway. Finally he closes the elevator door.

As they walk toward the suite, Alexandre fills Borelli in on the details.

ALEXANDRE: Not the slightest surprise. A completely predictable moment. She takes herself to be a great lover, while in reality she's a middle-class lady from the sticks. With pretensions of culture. There's nothing worse!

They reach the door to Alexandre's suite. Borelli takes out a key and opens it.
They enter the living room. Alexandre sheds his suitcoat.

ALEXANDRE: I started off by saying—to shake her up a bit—"Off with your clothes! Except for the jewelry. I want to take a good look at you!"

Alexandre unties his tie.

ALEXANDRE: All of which simply set her to clucking like a hen. And then she started reciting Baudelaire to me. That was the last straw.

Alexandre picks up his suitcoat, takes a paperback—a detective story—from the outside pocket, and tosses it over to Borelli, who catches it in mid-air.

ALEXANDRE: Fortunately, she's a nut for detective stories. Which gave me a subject of conversation to help conceal my lack of, how shall we say, appetite?

Borelli glances at the cover of the book.
Suddenly, Alexandre's expression changes. His face lights up with a kind of childish joy. He starts going through his suitcoat pockets. From one he takes out a fat wad of banknotes, which he places on the table. Then he brings out the superb antique necklace the young woman was wearing around her neck that morning in the hotel lobby.
Alexandre walks over toward Borelli, dangling the necklace before him. Borelli seems flabbergasted. It's not as though he hadn't seen his share of Alexandre's conquests, but still!

ALEXANDRE: She has no notion of how much this is worth! She gave it to me for a song. The silly goose is married to a miserly old man, so she needs money for her extra-marital escapades!

At which point Borelli is overcome with an uncontrollable fit of laughing. He looks at the necklace, takes it in his hand, and

49

studies it with a knowledgeable eye, still shaking with laughter.

Apparently his laughter is contagious, for Alexandre is by now laughing just as hard.

But then, just as suddenly as he began, Borelli stops laughing. Again he looks at the necklace, then at Alexandre. When he speaks again, his tone of voice has changed completely:

BORELLI: Alex!

Alexandre has sensed that the change of tone implies something important, and as he turns around he is frowning.

BORELLI: I've gone through the books, Alex. And I might as well tell you: they're a disaster.

Alexandre starts to speak but Borelli stops him.

BORELLI: Let me have the floor, Alex, just once! After I've said my piece you can add whatever you want. But I want to have my say first!

Alexandre yields. He sits down. Borelli takes a little black notebook from his pocket. When Alexandre sees it he gets to his feet with a smile on his face, goes over to his jacket, and gets a little notebook bound in red leather. He goes back over and sits down in the same chair.

Both he and Borelli look at each other, as though they were about to compete in some game.

ALEXANDRE: Ready! Let's see if your bookkeeping coincides with mine!

Borelli shakes his head as he leafs through his notebook.

BORELLI: The racing stable: three million francs' loss. Is that what you have?

Alexandre checks his notebook and nods assent.

BORELLI: The Théâtre de l'Empire . . . I'm referring only to last season: a net loss of 6,237,378 francs. I'll throw in the centimes as a gift. . . .

ALEXANDRE: I never count the centimes anyway. . . .

Borelli glances at him, then goes on:

BORELLI: . . . Six hundred thousand francs paid out to the scandal sheets . . . three and a half million more down the drain in the advertising scheme . . . another two million gone for fees, payoffs, tips, and the like to your lawyers, congressmen, retired generals, government administrators and their ilk. . . .

Alexandre starts to interrupt, but Borelli asks for a minute more and proceeds:

BORELLI: I'm almost finished, Alex. Losses at the casinos: two million, two hundred fifty thousand at Biarritz . . . five million at Cannes. Grand total: twenty-two million francs squandered in less than two years!

Alexandre gets to his feet and begins pacing the floor, holding his little red notebook in his hand.

ALEXANDRE: Squandered! You have it all wrong, Borelli. Those millions weren't squandered. They were invested!

He pauses in front of Borelli.

ALEXANDRE: The only way to attract money is to show it . . . make a display of it. All my operations are based on credit. . . . And where do you think my credit comes from? From the life I lead, that "squandering" you refer to! If I stopped spending my money in public people would begin to grow distrustful. Alexandre must not be doing very well, they'd start to say, and that would be the end of it.

BORELLI: But the fact is your business *is* in trouble, Alex. . . . In two months you're going to have to appear in court.

ALEXANDRE: Véricourt has a plan all worked out. . . . We're going to work out an arrangement with the plaintiffs. . . .

BORELLI: Work out an arrangement! That's what we're always doing, working out arrangements! And where do you think you're going to come up with the money to make these arrangements you're talking about?

Alexandre does not reply. Borelli doesn't let go.

BORELLI: And what about the Bayonne bonds? A week ago, three million francs' worth came up for redemption. . . . You couldn't pay them off. A month from now another five million fall due. . . . If there's any kind of investigation they'll also find out that your Bayonne bonds are phony!

Alexandre stops him with an irritated gesture.

ALEXANDRE: The fact is I do need one hundred million. That I'm not denying. But in two months the International Monetary and Development Fund will be operative! With the five hundred million that will raise I'll pay off the outstanding Bayonne bonds, and we'll be free and clear again, my dear Borelli!

Borelli almost appears convinced. He nonetheless raises one last objection.

BORELLI: And meanwhile? What are you going to do, your "emerald number"?

The mere mention of the "emerald number" sends both of them off into paroxysms of laughter.

ALEXANDRE: I have a much better plan than that, my friend. Involving our hidalgo . . . He's madly in love with Arlette. . . . He'll listen to what I have to say. . . .

Borelli, pursing his lips and obviously disgusted by the very thought of any plan involving Montalvo, says:

BORELLI: Montalvo? He's nothing but a polo player, a drawing-room revolutionary! . . .

ALEXANDRE: Don't be too sure. . . . He's preparing a *coup d'état* in Spain. . . . He's trying to buy arms from Mussolini. And when you're operating on that level you need a lot of money. It occurred to me that my company in Geneva would provide a perfect cover for him, a place where he could deposit his funds. . . .

Obviously, Alexandre has seized on a simple remark that Baron Raoul made earlier in the day, about Montalvo's trip to Italy, and already blown it up into a full-scale project.

16.

The Place Saint-Georges in Paris. The time is 8:00 p.m., July 24, 1933.

Alexandre is getting out of his limousine before 28 Place Saint-Georges. He is dressed in a tuxedo, and draped over his shoulders is an elegant evening cape.

He goes into the building, which houses the offices of his various companies. Turning on the lights as he goes, he makes his way up through the floors of the building, which at this time of night is empty. We follow him as he goes up a stately staircase and into a large room that doubtless serves for board meetings.

Alexandre looks out over the vast, empty room. Then, suddenly, he moves quickly across the room and picks up some massive chandeliers. He lights the candles, turns off the electric lights, and places the chandeliers on one end of the long table covered with green baize.

He takes up a position at the head of the table and, resting his hands on the back of the chairman's chair, begins a solitary speech:

ALEXANDRE: Your excellencies, gentlemen, my dear friends! I am happy to welcome you to this the first meeting of the International Monetary and Development Fund!

He is caught up in his own game. He looks around the room as though he were really addressing a meeting of the board.

ALEXANDRE: One question, and one question alone, haunts the period through which we're living, and that is: what must we do to extricate ourselves from the present economic crisis?

He pauses to make his effect. Then:

ALEXANDRE: Hard as it is to believe, what we are witnessing today in the most advanced countries of the world is the following paradox: on the one hand, mountains of unsold merchandise, and on the other vast numbers of people who have been thrown out of work!

He peers into the semi-darkness around him.

ALEXANDRE: What is the root of this evil situation? Today . . .

As he pronounces this word, a bell rings somewhere in the building.

Alexandre looks to see what time it is. He leaves the board room, with the candles in the chandeliers still burning, and goes into his well-appointed offices. On the mantelpiece of the fireplace, a huge photograph of Arlette, bare-shouldered in a lovely evening dress.

Alexandre strides over to the far end of his office and pushes a button which releases a secret door.

Without a word of greeting, Inspector Boussaud enters the office.

17.

The Place Saint-Georges in Paris. The time is 8:30 p.m., July 24, 1933.

Borelli arrives at the Place Saint-Georges, but instead of entering the office building walks across the street and takes up a position in a gateway, from where he can keep a close eye on Alexandre's headquarters. As always he gives the impression of massive self-composure.

*

Once again, we isolate Borelli's face from the background in which we have just seen him, in a close-up shot.

When he speaks, his voice is precise and self-controlled.

BORELLI: I would like to clarify one important point, Mister

Chairman. . . . You said: his trusted friend. I wasn't his trusted *friend*, but his trusted *employee*. In his relationships with all his employees he was the boss, in the fullest sense of the term.

18.

The Place Saint-Georges in Paris. The time is 8:35 p.m., July 24, 1933.

Back in Alexandre's office, where Inspector Boussaud and Alexandre are in deep discussion. Alexandre is clearly upset by something that Boussaud has told him, and is pacing the floor while the Inspector follows him with his eyes.

ALEXANDRE: That's the last straw! I was promised that my file would be kept under lock and key! That no one would have access to it!

BOUSSAUD: Well, somehow Bonny has got hold of it. I saw it in his office with my own eyes. But there's nothing more Bonny can glean from it. He's already given *La Bonne Guerre* everything it contains.

ALEXANDRE: What worries me is what Bonny is dreaming up outside the framework of the *Sûreté.*

BOUSSAUD: I happen to know what he's dreaming up. He has a plan to do you in. He's going to spend the month of August in Biarritz, and while he's there he's going to hock some phony jewels at the Bayonne Municipal Pawnshop.

19.

The Place Saint-Georges in Paris. The time is 8:45 p.m., July 24, 1933.

In the darkened street, a small door opens and Inspector Boussaud emerges, having left Alexandre's offices by a secret exit.

Hidden in the recess of a doorway, Borelli observes Boussaud's departure. Then he crosses the street and goes into the building, arriving in Alexandre's personal office by the same secret route that Boussaud has just taken. Alexandre is in the adjoining bathroom, carefully massaging his face with a beauty cream, in front of a mirror. He speaks without turning toward Borelli.

ALEXANDRE: Did you see him leave?

BORELLI: Yes.

ALEXANDRE: Nothing unusual. No one followed him?

BORELLI: No.

Alexandre emerges from the bathroom. He slips on his tuxedo jacket.

ALEXANDRE: What a rat's nest, the so-called vice squad. It's just as corrupt as police headquarters itself! I must speak to Véricourt about it. He should sponsor a law in the House revamping the whole police setup!

Borelli's expression indicates total agreement. Alexandre picks up his hat.

ALEXANDRE: You know what Bonny has dreamed up? He's going to spend his vacation in Biarritz . . . leaving a few days from now. And he's going to set a trap for me. He's going to hock some phony jewelry at the Bayonne Municipal Pawnshop, as a means of subsequently starting an investigation.

BORELLI: Bonny's not as dumb as he looks!

But Alexandre's expression indicates that his mind has already moved on to another subject.

ALEXANDRE: I have a mad desire to go wake up Arlette! To be in Biarritz tomorrow morning!

BORELLI: But Baron Raoul is waiting to have dinner with us.

ALEXANDRE: I know. Let's go pick him up. We'll drive all night. . . . You all set?

Borelli's mimed reply indicates that he is always ready . . . for anything.

20.

A country inn somewhere in the south of France. The time is 11:15 p.m., July 24, 1933.

Inspector Gardet appears on the stairway of a country inn in the Gironde region of southern France, and walks down the hallway.

In front of the door to one of the rooms, a blond, blue-eyed, Nordic-looking young man is seated, obviously guarding the room. He is one of Trotsky's secretaries.

As he passes, Inspector Gardet nods ever so slightly to the young man, who hardly returns the greeting. The young man watches the Inspector as he disappears down the hallway.

21.

Biarritz. The time is 6:00 a.m., July 25, 1933.

Alexandre's limousine, its motor turned off, glides as in a dream down a hill toward the ocean.

We can hear the muffled sound of breakers, and in the gray light of dawn the silver gleam of the water in the distance.

Here and there, the first touches of pink in the sky.

After an all-night drive, the three men have reached Biarritz just as dawn is breaking.

The chauffeur puts on the brakes and the limousine comes to a gentle halt.

Borelli, who is seated next to the chauffeur, stretches, then opens his door. Alexandre is out of the car. In the gray-pink light of early day he is walking toward the ocean. In the back seat, Baron Raoul is still dozing.

Alexandre looks out over the ocean, then over the country-side for a long moment, before turning and heading back toward the car. He goes up to Borelli, who is standing beside the car's long, sleek hood, and says:

ALEXANDRE: Let's go buy some flowers!

Borelli looks at him without the slightest expression. The Baron emerges from his half-sleep to say:

BARON RAOUL: Flowers, Sacha, at six in the morning!

Alexandre turns aside the objection with an irritated gesture of his hand.

ALEXANDRE: Six in the morning, midnight, I don't care what time it is. I want flowers for Arlette, a mountain of white flowers. We'll go drag the florists from their beds, if necessary. I want lilies, orchids, camellias, roses!

Borelli remarks laconically to Alexandre's effusion:

BORELLI: White roses are pretty.

22.

Biarritz. The time is 8:00 a.m., July 25, 1933.

A street in Biarritz. The limousine is parked in front of a

florist shop, whose owners, still in their night clothes, are help-
ing Baron Raoul and Borelli literally load the car with white
flowers of every kind and description.

Alexandre is peeling off banknotes, paying the bewildered
florists, who obviously have been literally dragged from their
beds to make the sale.

Borelli is staring at the flower-filled limousine. As it starts off,
the three men—Alexandre, Baron Raoul, and Borelli—follow on
foot as it moves down the main driveway toward the Palace
Hotel.

23.

The Hôtel du Palais in Biarritz. The time is 8:30 a.m., July
25, 1933.

Alexandre is in Arlette's suite at the hotel. He, with the help of
a whole army of bellhops, is arranging the floral displays in her
living room.

When they have finished, Alexandre sends them on their way, distributing more-than-generous tips to each as they file out.

In the bedroom, Alexandre gazes at Arlette, who is still fast asleep. His expression, perhaps because of the passionate concentration, is frozen, somehow pained.

Silently, Alexandre has been filling up Arlette's bedroom with the baskets of flowers, until the whole floor is covered with them, and the furniture, too. Even the bed itself.

It looks almost like an altar.

Still wearing his tuxedo, Alexandre has lain down on the bed next to Arlette. Both their heads are crowned with white flowers, their bodies are as though covered with a winding sheet of white flowers.

Alexandre takes out the necklace that he purchased a few hours before from the silly provincial woman for a mere pittance, and carefully fastens it around Arlette's neck. She opens her eyes at the touch and, seeing the snowdrift of flowers, cries out.

Then she turns her head, sees Alexandre, and throws her

arms around his neck.

ARLETTE: Sacha!

They are both lying back against the pillows now, their heads close together.

ARLETTE: I had that same bad dream again.

ALEXANDRE: I know.

ARLETTE: The car was driving at first on the grass . . .

ALEXANDRE: We were together?

ARLETTE: Yes, you were holding me in your arms. I could hear your voice in my ear.

ALEXANDRE: The same words as always?

ARLETTE: Yes, the same . . . Ermine, orchids . . . Your voice in my ear . . .

ALEXANDRE: The car kept going faster and faster?

ARLETTE: Faster and faster, down the slope . . .

Her voice grows more and more desperate, and her words tumble out.

ARLETTE: . . . We were falling into a precipice, the car flew away into a cloud of white feathers . . . no, it was a snow cloud, I was having trouble breathing, and I could no longer see your face . . . there was snow everywhere, as far as the eye could see. . . .

By this time Arlette is almost shouting. Alexandre claps his hand over her mouth.
He gets up, strides over to the windows, pulls back the curtains and lets the bright sunlight stream into the room.

ALEXANDRE: There, you see: there's no snow, Arlette. Only sunlight. Bright July sunlight. We're happy, Arlette.

She begins to relax slightly. She looks down at the necklace that Alexandre has fastened around her neck.

62

ARLETTE: It's beautiful. Where did you get it?

Alexandre bursts out laughing—a mixture of childish pleasure and male self-assurance.

ALEXANDRE: Yesterday, at ten o'clock in the morning, this necklace was gracing the neck of a young lady from the fair town of Angoulême, who was seated in the lobby of the Claridge. At five in the afternoon, I was in the young lady's bed. A plump morsel, lovely skin, and thoroughly depraved; but without a brain in her head! By seven last evening the necklace was snug in my pocket!

Arlette laughs, the laugh of an accomplice, with an undertone of vulgarity.

ARLETTE: Did you make her pay you to go to bed with her?

Alexandre seems to appreciate her remark, which he apparently finds very witty.

ALEXANDRE: I didn't stoop that far! But I did manage to come away with that necklace for a tenth of its real value.

Arlette looks at Alexandre, and in her look is both submission and ardent devotion.

ARLETTE: Come!

63

Alexandre glances toward the door.

ARLETTE: The maids will be arriving any minute. . . . But I don't care!

He takes a step or two toward the bed.

24.

The Municipal Pawnshop in Bayonne. The time is 3:30 p.m., July 25, 1933.

Alexandre arrives at the front door of the Municipal Pawnshop in Bayonne. From a viewpoint outside the building, we see him enter and go up to an office on the second floor. Then, inside, we see him talking with Gauthier, the director of the Pawnshop.

GAUTHIER: Three million francs' worth, Alex. Three million francs' worth of bonds that are due and that we haven't paid off. If the tax inspector notices that the numbers of

those bonds don't correspond to anything in my books, I've had it! It's too risky. . . . You have to pay them off!

Alexandre gets to his feet and makes a gesture meant to minimize the scope of the problem.

ALEXANDRE: The tax people won't notice a thing! They've been auditing you now for two years, right? So stop worrying! I'll be sending you the money within a week! . . .

He heads for the door but pauses before he exits and turns back to Gauthier.

ALEXANDRE: But look out for Inspector Bonny! That's the only thing you have to worry about. . . .

25.

The casino in Biarritz. The time is 4:30 p.m., July 25, 1933.

A gaming room in the Biarritz casino. Afternoon. A broad bay window looks out onto the ocean beach.
    Alexandre and Baron Raoul appear near the bay window.

ALEXANDRE: How does it feel, Baron, to have squandered a fortune like yours?

BARON RAOUL: A feeling of complete satisfaction, Sacha, the only real feeling of complete satisfaction a man can have.

They leave the proximity of the bay window and make their way among the gaming tables. The casino is relatively quiet in the afternoon, but at several tables various fairly subdued games are going on. Alexandre takes a few chips from his pocket.

BARON RAOUL: One of my ancestors conquered Europe for Napoleon. His descendents conquered the stock market, industry, and colonial commerce, and built up an enormous fortune. And I, Sacha, have managed to run through that infamous fortune in one long party. It took me more than forty years to do, but I finally succeeded!

ALEXANDRE: How I would have liked to be in your shoes. My

problem is that I have to keep reinventing the fortunes I squander. . . . I hadn't a penny to my name to start with!

At the gaming table closest to where they are standing the croupier is calling out the next round.

CROUPIER: Place your bets, Gentlemen. The house bets ten thousand francs. Place your bets!

ALEXANDRE: I'll match the house. Some cards, please . . .

CROUPIER: Nine for the bank, and baccarat!

Alexandre watches the croupier scoop in the chips. He has lost his whole pile.

ALEXANDRE: You see, Baron, it's high time we left Biarritz.

And on those words they leave the gaming room.

26.

The Parma Airport in Biarritz. The time is 5:15 p.m., July 25, 1933.

Juan Montalvo's Hispano-Suiza is silently driving along, followed by Alexandre's Rolls Royce. Both cars drive into the grassy area which constitutes the Parma Airport in Biarritz. At the far end of the field sits one of those planes which in the 1930s carried the mail. Both cars head for the plane and stop, and five passengers emerge.

Arlette, Baron Raoul, and Borelli walk on ahead, while Alexandre takes Montalvo aside, a short distance away from the others.

ALEXANDRE: So, Montalvo, how is your *coup d'état* progressing in Spain. Did Mussolini agree to sell you any arms?

Montalvo is taken aback. He gives a start, but Alexandre hastens to reassure him.

ALEXANDRE: Don't worry, my lips are sealed.

MONTALVO: But who in the world told you? . . .

ALEXANDRE: No one. I figured it out for myself. I heard you talking to the Baron about a trip to Italy. So I simply put two and two together. . . .

MONTALVO: Your deductive powers are most impressive!

Alexandre flashes a smile, obviously pleased with himself.

ALEXANDRE: As you know, the sale and purchase of arms on an international scale is a very tricky business, involving as it does large transfers of money. Discretion is the prime requisite, don't you agree? You need a sure place to keep your money in escrow during the negotiations. It so happens that I have a company in Geneva, and a bank account in the Union of Swiss Banks. . . .

As he says these words, Arlette, who is walking ahead with Baron Raoul and Borelli, turns around and looks back at them.

MONTALVO: Your kind offer couldn't come at a better time. In fact, I was just in the process of trying to find a solution to that very problem!

Alexandre and Montalvo saunter over and rejoin the others.

27.

Saint-Palais-sur-Mer, on the French Riviera. The time is 6:00 p.m., July 25, 1933.

As dusk falls, the two-car Trotsky convoy makes its way along a road which parallels the sea.
　　We see a road sign which reads: SAINT-PALAIS-SUR-MER.
　　The lead car, bearing Trotsky, his wife, and his secretaries, pulls up in front of a villa, called Les Embruns—*which means "spray" or "spindrift." The second car, Inspector Gardet's, pulls up and parks a short distance away.*
　　Inspector Gardet has emerged from his car. We see, from

Gardet's viewpoint, the silhouette of Trotsky as he, still dressed all in white and leaning on the arm of his wife, Natalia, makes his way into the house. The secretaries begin to take down the baggage.

For a few moments, Inspector Gardet observes the scene. Then he climbs back into his car.

28.

The Hôtel Claridge in Paris. The time is 7:00 p.m., July 27, 1933.

Alexandre's suite in the Claridge. Through the tall windows that overlook the Champs-Élysées, we see that night is falling. We make a rapid tour of the suite, the camera moving from one room to the next. In the master bathroom, Alexandre is exercising. In the bedroom, a chambermaid is laying out clothing for the evening, both male and female.

In the living room, Baron Raoul and Arlette are chatting.

The Baron is already in tuxedo, but Arlette still has on an after-noon gown.

BARON RAOUL: Do you remember that American lady, Mrs. Winters? The one who had the face lift? She looked for all the world like a doll. I'm sure you ran into her in Monte Carlo. . . . Anyway, she always carried a mirror with her, wherever she went, even when she was out walking. Carried it in her hand, in fact. Well, the other day her whole world fell apart. She couldn't bear the way she looked to herself: old age kept showing through the face lift. She slashed her wrists . .·. in her bathtub. . . .

Nervously, in a voice that betrays concern, Arlette stops him.

ARLETTE: Please don't tell Sacha that story, Baron. Not today. It's an anniversary!

The Baron looks at her quizzically, surprised by the force of her tone.

ARLETTE: You're a good friend, I can tell you why. . . . It was seven years ago today that Sacha's father committed suicide. . . . Oh, some family tragedy brought it on. Sacha was away . . . on a business trip.

Clearly sympathetic, Baron Raoul takes Arlette's hand.

BARON RAOUL: I'm terribly sorry! I didn't know. You can count on my discretion, my dear Arlette!

As he reassures her, we hear the sound of footsteps. Arlette withdraws her hand from the Baron's and composes herself.
Alexandre enters the room. He is thin, young looking, in very good physical shape. But his face reveals that he is wrestling with some inner demon.

ALEXANDRE: Ah, Baron, you're already here! I'm delighted. Tonight we're going to celebrate!

And he laughs, challenging fate, provoking it.

29.

A Russian nightclub in Paris. The time is 11:30 p.m., July 27, 1933.

The party is seated at a long table in a Russian nightclub with all that such a place implies: gypsy music, violins, Russian dances.
Covertly, Arlette is watching Alexandre with great tenderness. It becomes apparent that Alexandre is very drunk. He is seated between Baron Raoul and a former police prefect, Monsieur Houriaux. Also at the table, seated not far from Alexandre, is Dr. Mézy, who like Arlette seems to be keeping a close eye on him.

ALEXANDRE: . . . You know, Oscar Wilde hit the nail on the head when he said: "There's nothing worse than prison."

BARON RAOUL: But he's wrong, Sacha! There is something worse than prison, and that's death!

The Baron is joking, but Alexandre is dead serious.

ALEXANDRE: And I say prison is worse than death!

The retired police prefect interrupts:

HOURIAUX: What do we know of such matters, my friend? None of us here has had any experience either with death or prison.

ALEXANDRE: I do. I've had experience with prison.

Houriaux and the Baron both laugh at what is obviously Alex's little joke. But of course he is not joking; drink has stripped him of his usual self-control. Or perhaps he enjoys playing with fire.

HOURIAUX: You forget, my friend, that I'm an ex-prefect of police. If that were true, I would know. And since I don't . . .

He laughs, clearly pleased with his powers of deduction. Alexandre looks at Houriaux, and in that glance we have a feeling that he is on the verge of opening his mouth and suddenly revealing the whole truth, of spilling the past he usually tries so hard to forget.

ALEXANDRE: No! You don't know anything about me! No one knows who I am, or what I'm capable of!

Alexandre freezes, his glass of vodka in his hand. He is beside himself with anger. Suddenly he sets down his glass and leaves the table.

Arlette and Dr. Mézy exchange looks. Then, very calmly, Dr. Mézy gets to his feet and follows Alexandre.

30.

The Père-Lachaise Cemetery in Paris. The time is midnight, July 27, 1933.

Alexandre, his evening cape floating behind, is walking among the tombstones of the Père-Lachaise Cemetery. He is walking quickly and with a sure step: he knows exactly where he is going.

Alexandre reaches an impressively large tombstone on whose black marble surface no name is engraved. He lies down full length on the gravestone and remains there in total silence for a few seconds.

Then we hear the crunch of gravel as footsteps approach, and we see two legs loom into Alexandre's field of vision. Alexandre lifts his head: it is Dr. Mézy standing over him.

ALEXANDRE: The day he found out that I was stealing the gold for his fillings and prosthetic devices, he said to me: "Sacha, if ever you dishonor the family name, I warn you I'll kill myself."

Alexandre is speaking very calmly. Dr. Mézy sits down on the gravestone, near Alex's head, and listens to the rest of his story.

ALEXANDRE: Honor, work: I swear those seemed to be the only two words he knew. As though they had honored or respected his name at the time of the pogroms! But he wanted to forget all that, he wanted people to think of him as a decent, hard-working dentist of the decent, upper-class sixteenth arrondissement!

He laughs derisively but quietly. Dr. Mézy says nothing, waiting for what is to follow:

ALEXANDRE: And I also swear that if it hadn't been for my grandfather, who kept poking fun at him, he would have gone to mass every Sunday!

Suddenly he is overcome by an access of fury, of childish anger. He slams his fist down on the gravestone.

ALEXANDRE: Is there anything worse in the world than having a faint-hearted father?

Dr. Mézy lays a friendly, calming hand on Alexandre's shoulder. For a few seconds neither one speaks. Then:

ALEXANDRE: And yet he did find the courage to fire a bullet into his head!

At that point, a man arrives, holding a lantern in his hand. It's the guardian of the cemetery.

GUARDIAN: You must leave, Gentlemen. I've already let you stay longer than I should have. . . .

31.

The Père-Lachaise Cemetery in Paris. The time is 12:15 a.m., July 28, 1933.

At the cemetery gate, Arlette is waiting for Alexandre in a black limousine.

Alexandre gets into the car, where Arlette greets him and helps him stretch out on the back seat, with his head on her knees. She soothes him and treats him with the tenderness and understanding one would show a child, someone whose heart has been broken. In the tiny vases that grace both sides of the richly upholstered back seat, we note that there are some white flowers.

32.

A beach somewhere in Normandy. The time is 7:00 a.m., July 28, 1933.

Still dressed in their evening clothes, Arlette and Alexandre are

walking slowly along a Normandy beach in the pale light of dawn.

About ten yards behind them, the liveried chauffeur follows them, carrying a car blanket over his arm.

33.

Saint-Palais-sur-Mer. The time is 11:00 a.m., on an unspecified day in August.

The warm skies of August in the south of France near the sea. We see the town post office, which faces a small square.

Inspector Gardet emerges from the post office and descends the steps to the sidewalk, where he climbs onto a bicycle and rides off.

Astride the bike, looking a bit awkward as he sits in his summer outfit, straight backed and somewhat stiff, Inspector Gardet pedals steadily along the road that runs by the sea, until he reaches the house where Trotsky is staying, Les Embruns.

He sets down his bicycle and walks into the grounds surrounding the house. Before he gets very far, two young men who look as though they can handle most any situation appear out of nowhere. Each of them has one hand in his coat pocket. One of them has pulled out his hand to the point where we can actually see that it is clasping a gun.

Unruffled, the Inspector continues on his way. The two men recognize who the intruder is and stop in their tracks. One of them retraces his steps, apparently to resume what he had been doing prior to Gardet's arrival, and disappears behind the house.

Gardet is standing on the edge of the lawn now, talking to one of Trotsky's secretaries, the blue-eyed one with the Germanic look whom we have seen before.

GARDET: Everything O.K.? Nothing out of the ordinary to report?

The Secretary shakes his head.

GARDET: Tell me, am I right in assuming you don't get any mail?

The Secretary's fleeting smile is tinged with irony.

SECRETARY: You're not suggesting that it would be wise or prudent to have letters sent to Monsieur Leon Trotsky, General Delivery, Saint-Palais-sur Mer, are you? That would hardly be circumspect!

Still unruffled, Inspector Gardet goes on.

GARDET: And yet Monsieur Trotsky does receive a great many visitors. . . . English political figures . . . Belgian . . . not to mention a great many extreme Left Wing German refugees. . . .

Gardet glances past the Secretary to the other side of the lawn.

SECRETARY: Of course he does! And if they come to see Monsieur Trotsky, one can safely presume they are Left Wing!

GARDET: What I meant was, politically *involved* in extreme Left Wing movements!

The Inspector stresses the word "involved." Again he glances past the Secretary to where Trotsky is stretched out on a chaise longue, his legs covered with a blanket. His wife, Natalia, is reading to him aloud. Both of them are protected from the sun by a parasol. On a nearby table, a samovar.

GARDET: I'm sure I don't need to remind you, Monsieur, that one of the conditions agreed to by Monsieur Trotsky, as part of his being granted the right of asylum, was that he would strictly abstain from any involvement in French politics. . . .

SECRETARY: German refugees are involved in German politics. . . .

GARDET: But the fact is they are involved in it on French soil! That's the rub, Monsieur!

34.

The Saint-Palais-sur-Mer beach. The time is 11:30 a.m., on an unspecified day in August 1933.

Michel Grandville and Erna Wolfgang are at the beach, seated on the rocks. Without any prior explanation as to why or how Michel and Erna happen to know each other, we see them together.

GRANDVILLE: They need a German secretary for a few days. . . . I spoke to them about you. . . . In principle, it's all set. . . . I'll be going over to their house in a little while and I'll take you along with me.

ERNA WOLFGANG: Have you been there often? What's it like?

GRANDVILLE: Have you read Dostoevski? If you have, you have some idea of the life they lead: it's straight out of a Dostoevski novel: a very austere, but very rich and exciting life!

*

A series of shots appear one after the other on the screen. In the first, we see Trotsky and Natalia inside the house, entertaining a number of people, Grandville among them.

In the next shot, Trotsky and his wife are walking hand in hand in the first light of morning—or it may be evening—along a deserted beach, followed at a certain distance by two secretary-bodyguards.

In the third shot, it is night: Trotsky appears on the front steps of his house, and as he does the lights of a moving car suddenly strike him so that he looks like some white ghost protecting his eyes from the headlights with his right hand. The headlights are turned off. In the semi-darkness, a thin, nimble-footed silhouette moves quickly toward Trotsky. The men shake hands, and their handclasp is long and friendly.

Over these last shots we hear Michel Grandville's voice again.

GRANDVILLE (voice over): . . . and then Malraux came to pay him a visit. . . . Now there's one conversation I would have loved to overhear!

*

Back at the Saint-Palais-sur-Mer beach. Erna is listening to Grandville's account.

GRANDVILLE: From what Rudolf reports, they talked about art, cinema, about Tukhachevski's Polish campaign, about the Red Army, Christianity. Simply that and nothing more!

ERNA WOLFGANG: Do you think Trotsky will be able to pull it off? You think he can ever have an influence on the Party again?

Grandville's expression darkens as his thoughts move from the undeniable but abstract intellectual pleasures to the harsh political realities of the situation.

GRANDVILLE: That, indeed, is the question! . . . Trotsky's every waking thought and deed has the Party as its focal point: influence the Party, transform the Party, reconstruct the Party. . . . On the one hand, Trotsky declares unequivocally that Stalin has betrayed the revolution. But on the other, there's no escaping the fact that the Party backs Stalin. So we come to the ineluctable contradiction: how can you wield any influence on an instrument you no longer control?

ERNA WOLFGANG: In that case, what are we all fighting about?

GRANDVILLE: Because nothing is foreordained. . . .

35.

Saint-Palais-sur-Mer. Noon of a day in August 1933.

A shot of Inspector Gardet riding a bicycle along the ocean. As he pedals along he passes two young people, also riding bicycles: Michel Grandville and Erna Wolfgang.

Inspector Gardet stops, turns, and watches them ride away. Then he continues on his way.

36.

The offices of the Sûreté générale in Paris. The time is 11:00 a.m., on a day in August 1933.

We are in a hallway in the Sûreté building. We see Inspector Gardet striding along, a file under his arm. Heading toward him in the hall is Inspector Bonny, as well turned-out as always.

The two men stop and shake hands.

GARDET: I thought you were away on vacation, Bonny.

BONNY: What about you?

GARDET: I have an appointment with the director. My vacation is a mixture of business and pleasure: the beach part time, and in between a rather secret and delicate mission!

Gardet's tone when he says this is half-joking, of course.

BONNY: That's my plan, too. . . . I'm leaving tomorrow for Biarritz, where I hope I'll be able to mix a little business with pleasure.

With these words, Bonny doffs his hat in a broad, theatrical gesture.

BONNY: My compliments, Chief Inspector Gardet!

Gardet chuckles and in like manner doffs his hat to Bonny.

GARDET: And mine to you, Chief Inspector Bonny!

Both men, heading in opposite directions, go on their separate ways.

37.

Biarritz and Bayonne. Various times and locations, on a day in August 1933.

The train station in Biarritz. We see Inspector Bonny emerging from a train.

Next we see Bonny talking with the porter of the Palace Hotel.

We pick him up later as he arrives in front of the Municipal Pawnshop of Bayonne. Then we see Bonny in Gauthier's office, offering him a collection of precious jewels housed in a jewel case.

We begin to hear Gauthier's voice over this last shot.

GAUTHIER (*voice over*): . . . That you, Borelli? This is Gauthier speaking. . . . I want you to tell Alex. The guy he warned me about has just been here to see me. . . . Yes, I recognized him right away, from the photos you showed me. . . .

Now Gauthier is alone in his office at the Municipal Pawnshop, talking into the phone.

GAUTHIER: He tried to pass off a whole lot of phony jewels. . . . No, of course not . . . I turned him down, but with kid gloves. He didn't notice a thing. I simply told him the Bayonne Pawnshop had attained its specified limit as far as jewelry was concerned and that we therefore couldn't legally take on any more. . . . Sounded very much on the up-and-up. . . .

38.

A doctor's office in Paris. The time is 9:30 a.m., November 19, 1933.

Alexandre is stretched out on a consulting-room bed. He is presumably undressed, for he lies there with his eyes closed with a sheet pulled up over him. He is wearing a mustache.

We are in the office of the eminent neurologist Professor Pierre, a medical authority on whom the law courts often call for expert opinions. Professor Pierre is fairly well along in years and appears a pillar of respectability. Seated at his desk, he is wearing a white medical blouse over his suit.

Standing beside him is Dr. Mézy. The two doctors are busy leafing through a medical file.

Suddenly the door to the doctor's office opens, and a nurse, or secretary, appears in the doorway.

NURSE: Professor! There's a man out here who insists on coming in! . . . He claims to be your patient's "advisor."

As she says the word "patient" she nods in the general direction of Alexandre. And it is clear from the way she utters the word "advisor" that that is the word the man in the outer office used when speaking with her, and that she has no clear idea as to what it might mean.

Professor Pierre seems annoyed by the intrusion.

PROFESSOR PIERRE: Out of the question! Tell him he'll have to wait! Anyway, we're almost finished with the examination.

The nurse closes the door behind her. The professor gets up and goes over to where Alexandre is lying. He is still in the same position we saw him in a minute or two ago, with his eyes closed.

PROFESSOR PIERRE: What's the meaning of this? You don't need a lawyer when you're in my office!

Suddenly Alexandre sits up, and as he does the sheet slips down, revealing a bare chest.

ALEXANDRE: But that's where you're wrong, Professor! I don't trust your conclusions!

Professor Pierre is flabbergasted. Alexandre pursues his line of reasoning.

ALEXANDRE: I know how these things work, Professor! One of the best ways of eliminating a competitor is to have him locked up. I have my share of enemies, and why shouldn't I? No one who is out to revamp the European monetary system can avoid making enemies!

Professor Pierre shakes his head. He glances over toward Dr. Mézy, who has come over to join them. When next he talks to Alexandre his voice is unctuous.

PROFESSOR PIERRE: And these enemies you're referring to, are they the same ones who stole the Eiffel Tower from you?

Alexandre's smile is indulgent.

ALEXANDRE: I know what you're thinking, Professor. You'd like me to believe that I'm a raving lunatic. First of all, I never said anyone stole the Eiffel Tower from me. I simply said that a *right* that I had bought and paid for—at a very steep price, I might add—was stolen from me: a monopoly on radio advertising broadcast from the Eiffel Tower radio station.

Alexandre lies back down and pulls the sheet up over him. Staring up at the ceiling, he goes on talking:

ALEXANDRE: But you'll see, I'm going to get it all back! I'm going to get the Eiffel Tower back!

Professor Pierre gives a slight shrug of his shoulders.

PROFESSOR PIERRE: You can get dressed now. . . . The examination is over.

On a piece of writing paper whose letterhead reads: "Professor Pierre, Neurologist. Accredited by the State Tribunals," we see a hand writing the date: November 19, 1933.
The Professor is again seated at his desk. He is discussing the results of his examination with Dr. Mézy. Alexandre is no longer in the room.

PROFESSOR PIERRE: Let's see . . . I first examined your patient in April 1931 . . .

DR. MÉZY: That's right. . . . And your initial diagnosis has been proved a hundred per cent correct. . . .

PROFESSOR PIERRE: Yes, it would certainly seem so. . . . The slow but certain evolution of generalized paralysis, with possible periods of temporary remission. . . . Whence the persecution complex . . . and his megalomania. . . .

DR. MÉZY: I assume we should continue with the malaria therapy you've perfected. . . .

The Professor nods in agreement. As the two men have been talking, he has kept on making notes.
At this point the door opens and Alexandre reappears. If we didn't know who it was we'd have trouble recognizing him. He is wearing a sad-looking, threadbare overcoat, beneath which we can see he has on a ready-to-wear suit. One has the feeling he is wearing a disguise. Unless the contrary is true, and this is the real person, whereas the elegant Alexandre we have seen till now is the disguise.
The Professor glances up at him.

PROFESSOR PIERRE: If you two gentlemen wouldn't mind stepping out into the waiting room—with Monsieur Stavisky's "advisor"—I'll write up your certificate immediately.

39.

Place Saint-Georges in Paris. The time is 10:45 a.m., November 19, 1933.

Alexandre, Dr. Mézy, and Borelli alight from a rented car and, using the back entrance that we have seen previously, go into the building that houses Alexandre's offices. It is a cold, bleak November day.

All three men enter Alexandre's private office by the secret door. On the mantelpiece, next to Arlette's photograph, is a vase filled with the red carnations that Alexandre seems to prefer.

Borelli crosses the office and exits through the leather-upholstered door.

Alexandre uncovers the door leading to his private bathroom, which also serves as a closet. He immediately begins to change his clothes, tossing the seedy-looking outfit he has been wearing onto the floor.

Dr. Mézy walks over to Alexandre's desk and places on the top the medical certificate that Professor Pierre has written. Then he picks up a magazine that is lying there. It's a magazine called Crapouillot; *the issue is dated March 1933, and the headline on the cover announces in bloody letters: "MYSTERIOUS DEATHS."*

As Dr. Mézy leafs through the magazine and at the same time carries on a conversation with Alexandre, the latter keeps appearing in his office, then disappearing back into the bathroom. Each time he comes into the office, he tosses another article of clothing onto the floor, until he has completely divested himself of his "Stavisky clothes" and reassumed his elegant self: Serge Alexandre, Financial Advisor. The following conversation takes place as Alexandre comes and goes.

DR. MÉZY: I didn't know you were so interested in "mysterious deaths."

ALEXANDRE: Not "deaths," not in the plural. What does interest me is the death of Loewenstein, the banker. . . . In many ways he was a man like me: a financial wizard.

DR. MÉZY: And what is it that concerns you about him, his suicide?

ALEXANDRE: Don't tell me you believe that cock-and-bull story about his suicide, Doc? Or that his death was accidental? He's flying in a plane over the English Channel and disappears, just like that! How simple it is. And I'm supposed to believe he fell out the plane window? No, my friend, it was a murder. His competitors did away with him. . . .

By the end of this speech, Alexandre has completely reverted to his old self, having also got rid of his false mustache. He strides over to the vase of carnations, picks one, and puts it in his buttonhole.

DR. MÉZY: Alex, you frighten me.

Alexandre turns around to Mézy, and we can see that he is on his guard for what may follow.

DR. MÉZY: I'm your doctor, Alex, but I'm also your friend. . . .

Alexandre nods for him to go on.

DR. MÉZY: You should take some time off, Alex. Turn your business over to Borelli and Grammont for a while and forget everything. Take Arlette and go away somewhere. . . .

Alexandre's reaction is one of anger.

ALEXANDRE: Leave? Now? Just when the International Monetary and Development Fund is almost ready? Without it, the whole thing crumbles. S.I.M.A., S.A.P.E.P., the Bayonne Municipal Pawnshop: I control them all, with my own two hands. . . .

DR. MÉZY: But that's just it, Alex. Isn't that too much for one man to control by himself? . . . Véricourt is worried. . . .

ALEXANDRE: Véricourt too? You mean Professor Pierre isn't the only one?

Just then the office door opens and Borelli come in with Grammont.

Borelli places four fat envelopes on Alexandre's desk. It doesn't take too much imagination to guess that they're all stuffed with banknotes. In addition to the envelopes, there is a piece of paper on which, in longhand, is the following list which we can read as though we were looking over Alexandre's shoulder:

1. Véricourt—25,000
2. La Volonté—25,000
3. La Liberté—15,000
4. Grammont—35,000

ALEXANDRE: The medical exam went off beautifully, Grammont!

While he is verifying the names and amounts on the piece of paper, Alexandre goes on talking to Grammont.

ALEXANDRE: Professor Pierre was of the opinion that I'm so crazy that it's out of the question for me to appear in court day after tomorrow. . . . But that's not the same as having all charges dropped, Grammont, which is what you promised!

Alexandre's tone is aggressive. Borelli, who is picking up the clothes that Alexandre has tossed on the floor, glances up at his boss, doubtless prompted by the menacing tone. But Grammont does not appear to be intimidated by Alexandre's aggressiveness. His reply is anything but submissive.

GRAMMONT: You're not stating the facts correctly. True, it was agreed that the plaintiffs would drop their charges. But to have them do so they had to be paid off. . . . I told you that with two million francs I could bring it off. Véricourt had the whole thing arranged. . . . But since July you've never been able to come up with those two million francs!

During Grammont's tirade, Borelli has disappeared, carrying the bundle of old clothes.

Alexandre's tone of voice drops a peg or two. As he says the following, he pushes a buzzer marked MESSENGER.

ALEXANDRE: I've been having some troubles with the exchequer, Grammont, as you well know!

GRAMMONT: In Deauville this summer, you spent three times the amount we needed to settle that affair once and for all! No, Sacha, it wasn't that you didn't have the money, it's simply that you threw it away foolishly, that's all. . . .

Alexandre is looking down at the money-filled envelopes on the desk. He laughs and is on the verge of replying when the door opens and the messenger comes in. He's an odd-looking colorless man who sports a mustache. His name is Laloy.

Alexandre rises and hands him three of the four envelopes.

ALEXANDRE: I want you to deliver all three of these, Laloy.

Laloy takes the envelopes, then says:

LALOY: The board of directors of the International Monetary and Development Fund are all here, Monsieur.

Laloy exits, carrying the three envelopes. Alexandre checks his appearance in a mirror. He turns and tosses the fourth envelope to Monsieur Grammont.

ALEXANDRE: You're quite right, Grammont, I do throw my money away foolishly. . . .

And he leaves the office.

Grammont and Dr. Mézy are left alone in the office. Grammont, who has picked up his envelope, is furious. Dr. Mézy looks at him, but it's impossible to tell what he is thinking.

GRAMMONT: Were you able to reason with him?

DR. MÉZY: He doesn't want to listen. . . . He's sick.

GRAMMONT: Very sick.

The lawyer loses his temper. Alexandre's pointed insult has made him irascible.

GRAMMONT: Sick! I don't give a damn about his sickness. Somehow we have to neutralize him, Mézy! Otherwise he's going to drag us all down with him!

DR. MÉZY: Is it that serious?

GRAMMONT: He doesn't have a penny to his name!

*

Both men exchange looks. Then, by a technique we have seen before, the setting changes and our camera is focused in close-up on Dr. Mézy.

DR. MÉZY: Madness, Gentlemen, what is madness? It's not for me to say in this situation. But that Alexandre was a sick man, that he was very sick, there can be no doubt whatsoever. . . .

40.

The Place Saint-Georges in Paris. The time is noon, November 19, 1933.

We are in the main board room, which we have seen previously, when Alexandre began to make a speech to a nonexistent audience. Now the real board meeting of the International Monetary and Development Fund has just taken place, and is breaking up.

Among those present we note, in addition to Alexandre himself, Borelli, Baron Raoul, the ex-prefect of police Houriaux, and a fair number of other distinguished and much-decorated gentlemen whom we have never seen before.

Alexandre is standing with a sheaf of papers in his hand. Baron Raoul, Houriaux, and Borelli form a little circle around him.

HOURIAUX: Your idea for solving the unemployment problem is, quite simply, grandiose. . . . I congratulate you on it.

Obviously flattered, and very much in his element, Alexandre smiles broadly. But he fails to notice Borelli's eyes, which are fixed on him. A worried look.

ALEXANDRE: My dear prefect. What we plan to do, quite simply, is set the mechanisms of economic expansion so that they will once again function properly.

HOURIAUX: And how soon do you think that the Fund's initial bond issue will start trading on the stock exchange?

ALEXANDRE: Our international operations involving the Hungarian debentures are guaranteed by the Treaty of Trianon. . . . The Foreign Office will of course have to give its blessing, but that should be forthcoming in a matter of days. . . . I had a meeting about it with the general secretary for Foreign Affairs. . . .

As they talk, the group makes its way toward the door: Baron Raoul takes Alexandre by the sleeve and pulls him off to one side.

BARON RAOUL: I also want to congratulate you, Sacha! But I have a confession to make to you: I don't understand the first thing about these international monetary transactions. The Hungarian debentures are all Greek to me!

Alexandre, obviously in excellent humor, laughs at the Baron's confession.

ALEXANDRE: You don't have to understand them, Baron. All that's required is that you have faith in me!

BARON RAOUL: But that I do, Sacha, that I do!

Both men laugh.

*

Borelli and Alexandre are walking through the hallways of the Place Saint-Georges office building.
    Borelli opens a door, then stands back to let Alexandre enter the office. As he does, Alexandre can be heard to say, while with his now-familiar gesture he takes out his gold watch, to some business associate or politician whom we cannot see through the open door:

ALEXANDRE *(voice over)*: I'll give you five minutes, my friend! I'm very busy. . . . We're in the midst of getting the International Fund off the ground . . .

The end of Alexandre's sentence escapes us. Borelli has closed the leather-upholstered door and stands outside, waiting for his boss to finish and re-emerge.

*

Once again we move in on Borelli's impassive face, until we isolate it again from the present setting. Borelli begins to speak, in a fleeting, staccato-like manner.

BORELLI: His madness took the following peculiar form: he would have given anything to make sure people talked about him, whereas he should have given anything to make sure people forgot about him. . . .

Once again we see Alexandre and Borelli walking through the office hallways. This time they both go into another office, where a short, middle-aged man with a Dutch accent gets up to greet them. He is hugging a leather briefcase to his chest.

ALEXANDRE: You know, Van Straaten . . . for the time being I'm not buying any jewelry. . . . In fact, I may have some to sell. . . .

Van Straaten nods vaguely, presumably implying that he is aware of the situation Alexandre is describing.

94

VAN STRAATEN: I'm not asking you to buy. . . . I just want to leave these with you. . . . I give you a free hand to work out whatever deal you think would be most profitable for both of us!

Alexandre's eyes light up. He is clearly intrigued by Van Straaten's proposal.

ALEXANDRE: Let's take a look at the goods!

With a quick, deft movement, Van Straaten opens his briefcase and removes from it several leather jewel boxes, which he empties onto the table. A shimmering succession of obviously valuable jewels lie there in impressive array.

Alexandre bends over and looks at them, hardly able to contain his excitement.

He studies the jewels, and brings one or two up close to his eye for more thorough scrutiny.

Then, with a smile that one could describe, if this were a popular novel, only as diabolic, he begins to select the stones and, on the velvet cloth which surrounded them in Van Straaten's briefcase, arrange them in what appears to be some kind of order.

ALEXANDRE: I presume you are not at liberty to tell me where these stones came from.

Van Straaten rubs his hands together as he says:

VAN STRAATEN: No, this involves the greatest discretion. Absolute discretion, in fact. It involves an Oriental family of princely birth which doesn't want any publicity about the disposition of the jewels.

Alexandre's skillful hands quickly arrange the individual stones until they become a glittering necklace.

Alexandre lifts his eyes and looks at Van Straaten.

ALEXANDRE: The Rosenkrantz necklace, which very mysteriously disappeared when the seals were removed. The heirs are looking for it.

Van Straaten stares at the ghost-necklace and says nothing.

ALEXANDRE: These jewels can't be sold for several months! And even then they'll have to be sold one at a time. What I can do, Monsieur Van Straaten, is to dispose of them through a fence in London. It would be very risky, and therefore I'd keep the entire proceeds. You wouldn't receive any commission this time. . . .

Van Straaten remains silent. He looks up at Alexandre with an expression which seems to be a mixture of hate and admiration.
Once again Alexandre and Borelli are walking through the hallways of the office. Borelli is carrying Van Straaten's briefcase under his arm.

ALEXANDRE: I want you to go to London tomorrow, Albert. It's my birthday. . . .

He smiles smugly.

BORELLI: How much do you think I can get?

ALEXANDRE: At least a million francs. . . . That'll give me a little breathing room. . . . You see, Lady Luck hasn't abandoned me!

Borelli shakes his head. He too is looking at Alexandre with an expression that might be described as worried admiration.
Just then, as they are about to climb a stairway leading from one floor to another, a young man, whom an employee is trying to hold back, tries to collar Alexandre as he walks past.

YOUNG MAN: I have to see you, Monsieur Alexandre. I have something extraordinary to offer you!

Borelli asks if he should step in and take care of the Young Man, but with a movement of his hand Alexandre indicates that there's no need.

ALEXANDRE: Tell me what your proposition is.

YOUNG MAN: O.K. I've invented a machine which is going to revolutionize the medical profession. It's a machine which can be used to examine pregnant women, tell what sex the baby is going to be, and indicate its prenatal state of health.

I call it the "matriscope."

ALEXANDRE: And just where do I fit in?

YOUNG MAN: This machine actually exists. I mean a prototype
does. But now we need to put it into production. I thought
maybe you'd be interested in backing a company which
would hold world rights to the matriscope.

ALEXANDRE: How much do you need to get you started?

*The Young Man looks at Alexandre, hesitates for a moment,
then plunges ahead:*

YOUNG MAN: I figure that with ten thousand francs . . .

But Alexandre curtly cuts him off in mid-sentence.

ALEXANDRE: Stop right where you are, my friend. Ten thou-
sond francs is ridiculous. How do you expect to inspire any
confidence if you ask for so little money? If the matriscope
really exists, then it has to be worth millions! And if it

doesn't, you should make your story sound at least plausible. Ten thousand francs . . . it's just not plausible.

And with that Alexandre turns and leaves. The Young Man makes as if to reply, but Borelli takes him by the arm.

BORELLI: You've bothered Monsieur Alexandre enough!

Suddenly, Alexandre turns back to the Young Man.

ALEXANDRE: Matriscope! I like the name. O.K., you're on. I'll show you how to start a business.

41.

Outside of Paris, first in Montigny, then in Barbizon. The time is noon, November 20, 1933.

In the silver light of November, Alexandre's limousine drives slowly, *majestically down a country road, a liveried chauffeur at the wheel. In the car are Alexandre, Arlette, Baron Raoul, and Juan Montalvo.*

The limousine stops in front of a house that to all appearances is abandoned, on the outskirts of Montigny-sur-Loing. The chauffeur opens the door and Alexandre gets out by himself and walks toward the gate, which creaks as he opens it. He makes his way through the tall grass and underbrush of the neglected grounds.

Arlette, Baron Raoul, and Montalvo remain behind in the

car. Arlette watches her husband disappear.

BARON RAOUL: It's a charming place. Does Sacha intend to buy it?

Arlette glances desperately over toward the Baron, then begins to stammer:

ARLETTE: No. It was here that Sacha's father . . .

She says no more, but she has already said enough for the Baron to know what she's alluding to: it was here that Alexandre's father committed suicide.
He takes Arlette's hand in his.

BARON RAOUL: Do you think I ought to walk back there and join him?

ARLETTE: No, leave him alone. That's the way Sacha is.

Arlette disengages her hand and turns to Montalvo.

ARLETTE: I'm so pleased you came back up from Rome, Montalvo. . . . I especially wanted you to be here for Sacha's birthday.

Montalvo bows worshipfully in reply. Just then, the sound of the gate opening announces Alexandre's return to them.

*

A couple of hours later; the scene has shifted to a country inn not far from Barbizon.
The liveried chauffeur is polishing the limousine, which certainly doesn't seem to need it. Arlette and Baron Raoul appear in the doorway of the inn and begin to stroll down one of the forest roads, with the limousine driving slowly in their wake.

*

Back inside the inn, Montalvo and Alexandre are talking. Both men are smoking cigars.

MONTALVO: In about a month—I'd say about Christmas—we'll be ready to transfer the necessary funds to your Swiss account.

ALEXANDRE: Would it be indiscreet to ask you how large the sum you plan to deposit there will be?

MONTALVO: One million pounds sterling. . . .

Alexandre smiles broadly.

ALEXANDRE: My God! That's not a *coup d'état* you're planning. It's a full-scale civil war!

MONTALVO: And why not?

*

Alexandre and Montalvo have joined Arlette and the Baron on their stroll through the woods. All four are now walking down a road on the edge of the woods, with the sleek black limousine following a few yards behind.

ALEXANDRE: I'm growing old, Baron. Last year for my birthday they threw me a magnificent party at the Théâtre de l'Empire. . . . Do you remember?

By his expression it is clear the Baron indeed remembers the party.

ALEXANDRE: My problem is I've lost my zest for life. I don't enjoy things the way I used to. Don't I look for all the world like a little shopkeeper who has taken his wife to the country for lunch?

BARON RAOUL: No, Sacha, I'm sorry to disappoint you, but you'll *never* look like a shopkeeper!

Alexandre begins to play the buffoon. He climbs up on a tree trunk and begins to play the part of a shopkeeper.

ALEXANDRE: But you're wrong, Baron, absolutely wrong. I'll have a little store in some tiny seaside resort. Why not? In the evening, I'll take up my post on the threshold of my shop and watch the world go by, and no one will ever guess that the shadow in the doorway was once the Great Alexandre.

They all laugh appreciatively at his mime.

*

Arlette leads them back toward the car. She is the first to get in, followed by Montalvo. Just as Baron Raoul is about to follow, his eye catches someone across the street, a young woman who strikes him as familiar. It is Erna Wolfgang, who is standing on a street corner at the edge of the forest.

BARON RAOUL: Could it be? Or are my eyes deceiving me?

No, his eyes are not deceiving him. Alexandre, his attention caught by the Baron's questions, follows his gaze.

BARON RAOUL: You know who that is standing over there, Sacha? It's that little German girl from last summer.

Arlette and Montalvo lean out of the door of the car, obviously intrigued.

BARON RAOUL: Don't you remember, Sacha? You gave her her cues at the audition. You were the Ghost from *Intermezzo!*

Alexandre looks at Erna. Now he remembers, and a youthful smile crosses his face: a recollection of happiness and pleasure, fleeting but real.

Baron Raoul strides briskly across the street to where Erna is standing, and begins talking to her.

Arlette and Alexandre exchange pregnant looks.

*

We see Alexandre's limousine disappearing down the street. As it goes, a young man riding a bicycle pedals up to where Erna is waiting. He gets off his bike, and we see that it is Michel Grandville.

Grandville and Erna start to take a walk, Michel pushing his bicycle beside him by the handlebars.

*

The leafless forest of late autumn. Empty footpaths. A tangle of underbrush.

In the distance a couple appears, walking slowly through the trees: it is Trotsky and Natalia. Their progress is snail-like, and they both seem to be leaning on each other for support.

One of the secretaries we have seen before opens the gate leading to a house whose name is Ker Monique, situated on the edge of the forest.

Two German shepherds bound up to Natalia, who starts to pet them.

A lamp is lighted; it is coming up to dusk.

Inside the house, in the living room of the Ker Monique, a group of militants is seated around Trotsky and the ever-present samovar, listening to him talk. Among them we see Michel Grandville.

*

*Erna Wolfgang and Michel Grandville are walking in the forest,
in the vicinity of Barbizon. From time to time they pause, then
start off again, and we pause and walk with them.*

GRANDVILLE: Since the government authorized him to move to
Barbizon, Trotsky is better. He has started working again.
Do you know what he says? He says that because of the
nearby forest and the Communist League groups he's in
contact with, he has a feeling that he's back in Russia again
in the time of his youth, when everything was still possible,
when you had to make up everything as you went along. . . .
And then there are other times when he grows discouraged.
The other day he blurted out: "Old age is the most un-
expected thing that can happen to a man. You can antici-
pate virtually everything, but not old age!"

ERNA: A pretty depressing statement.

GRANDVILLE: Exile is a pretty depressing situation.

    *

*Alexandre's limousine is driving down a street near Barbizon,
with the leafless trees of autumn flashing by.*
    We begin to hear the Baron's voice over this shot.

BARON RAOUL *(voice over)*: Why, whenever I think back to that
sad story, in which all the characters come forward wearing
masks, as was Alexandre himself—Alexandre of the thousand names—why is it that it is always that day in November
that obsesses me?

*Baron Raoul's face is framed in a close-up, as he gazes out the
back window of the limousine. Then his face is isolated from
its former setting, and again the soundtrack changes as it has
before: a rustling of papers and the occasional coughing which
have signaled the start of all such previous scenes.*

BARON RAOUL: Perhaps because it was that day, for some strange
reason, that I first had the foreboding of Alexandre's end.
And yet, anyone who did not know us in the course of those
years has no idea of the exhilaration we felt every day, of
the pure joy we experienced. We were all just as old—or as

young—as Alexandre, and Arlette's solemn beauty—and when I mention that name I cannot refrain from adding how deplorable I find it to picture her today languishing in some sordid prison cell—Arlette's beauty warmed all our hearts. In Biarritz, Gentlemen, there is a shop whose name symbolizes for me that entire time: Biarritz-Happiness.

*

As Baron Raoul pronounces the word "Gentlemen" near the end of his testimony, the camera withdraws to reveal that we are in a room where the parliamentary committee investigating the Stavisky Affair is gathered.

The deputies are seated around a horseshoe-shaped table. The witness—in the present case, Baron Raoul—is standing, facing the chairman of the committee, who is flanked by his legal advisors and a court stenographer.

The Baron's final words have caused an uproar in the room, as various members react angrily.

The Chairman is about to call for order.

42.

Paris. The committee room where the hearings on the Stavisky

Affair are being conducted. The time is 11:00 a.m., April 17, 1934.

Over the protesting voices, the Chairman's voice can be heard, as he addresses himself to Baron Raoul.

CHAIRMAN: I must remind the witness of why he has been summoned here.

Baron Raoul looks genuinely surprised.

CHAIRMAN: This parliamentary commission has been named for the purpose of trying to elucidate an affair which resulted in several deaths on February sixth, and brought this country to the brink of civil war. I will not contest that what you have told us is full of verve, but you pointedly seem to be ignoring all its sordid aspects. . . .

BARON RAOUL: I am telling the truth as I know it, Sir.

The Baron's self-composure has not been ruffled by the Chairman's admonishment.

CHAIRMAN: We are taking for granted that you are telling us the truth. Or must I remind you that you are under oath? Therefore, let me ask you a few questions. . . .

The Chairman looks down at his notes.

CHAIRMAN: You first met Alexandre at the Biarritz casino in April of 1931. . . .

The Baron nods in agreement, then confirms verbally:

BARON RAOUL: That is correct, Sir.

CHAIRMAN: And having met him in the casino, it never came to your attention that he had been formally forbidden to gamble in any casino throughout France, in those days?

BARON RAOUL: Never, Sir! And I must add that I find that difficult to believe, even knowing what I know today!

Again his words provoke a certain amount of angry reaction on the part of several members of the committee. Baron Raoul

turns to them and stares them down haughtily. Then he con-
tinues:

BARON RAOUL: I have a hard time believing that, Gentlemen,
because for more than two years I saw Alexandre in any
number of casinos—Cannes, Biarritz, Deauville—and I always saw him greeted with open arms by the casino inspectors. I saw Alexandre playing baccarat with some of the
most notable personnages in France—politicians, captains
of finance and industry—and there was never a hint that
he was anything but their equal. That, Gentlemen, is why
I still find it hard to believe!

*This time the Baron's words draw a mixed reaction, some seem-
ing to approve of his words, others clearly doubting them. We
see shrugs and shakes and nods, and hear mutters and whispered
conversations. Then another deputy intervenes to question
Baron Raoul.*

DEPUTY: That was in April 1931, which is precisely when Alexandre became involved with the Bayonne Municipal Pawnshop and started issuing those false bonds which literally
flooded the country. . . . What can you tell us on that
subject?

BARON RAOUL: Nothing. I first heard of the Bayonne bonds three
months ago, when the scandal became public.

*Again, from the muttered reaction of some deputies, it is ap-
parent that they do not believe the Baron's words. He turns to
them and says:*

BARON RAOUL: Try and understand, Gentlemen, that in real
life things don't happen the way they do on stage. On stage
all artifices are possible. . . . But you must think of me as
Fabrice at Waterloo, Gentlemen: all I know is one little
segment of a vast jigsaw puzzle.

The Chairman interrupts to say:

CHAIRMAN: Monsieur Raoul, I see that we will not be able to
finish with your testimony this morning. . . . We will call

you back for further testimony at a subsequent meeting of the commission.

Baron Raoul bows, and leaves the room.

*

In the antechamber, a court usher holds his coat for him and then hands him his cane.

Several other people are waiting to be called before the commission. Among them we recognize Inspector Gardet.

Another witness is a Monsieur de La Salle, whom at this juncture we do not know. The Baron recognizes him, however, and starts over to greet him. But La Salle studiously avoids his gaze and buries himself in his newspaper, which is the Right Wing Le Matin.

Our camera moves in to frame, in a close-up, an article in Le Matin, editorializing on the discovery that Trotsky is living in Barbizon, and demanding that he be expelled from France.

At the same time as we see the article, we hear Monsieur de La Salle's voice reading key passages from it.

LA SALLE *(voice over)*: "Why should we be surprised at discovering the revolutionary agitator Trotsky living in Barbizon? When the government allows the Staviskian rabble to do whatever it wants, why shouldn't it do the same for the Bolshevik riffraff? . . . Can we at least hope that the present incident will force the government to clean up once and for all the international scum that is presently the shame of Paris?"

The Baron leaves the antechamber, while the Court Usher calls out the name of the next witness.

COURT USHER *(voice over)*: Chief Inspector Gardet!

Inspector Gardet gets to his feet.

43.

Paris. The same committee room. The time is 11:30 a.m., April 17, 1934.

Inside the committee room, Inspector Gardet is standing in the witness box facing the Chairman.

CHAIRMAN: And what date was that?

GARDET: The end of November 1933. I was then working on another case and received a call from the head of the investigative division. . . .

*

The scenes that Inspector Gardet's words evoke are now seen. We first see him entering an office in the Sûreté, carrying a file under his arm. He puts the file down on the commissioner's desk, but the latter shakes his head. That's not the case he's called Gardet about. The commissioner hands him a piece of paper, which in fact are his orders.

GARDET *(voice over)*: . . . The note said more or less the following: "Serge Alexandre, 28 Place Saint-Georges, Paris. In-

ternational Monetary and Development Fund. I hereby authorize you most urgently to make a thorough investigation of the above-named person, at the request of the Ministry of Foreign Affairs. . . ."

Inspector Gardet gets up and leaves the commissioner's office.

We see him back in his own office, where he places the file he has been carrying (without doubt the Trotsky file) under lock and key. Then Gardet pays a visit to the office where the police files are kept. At which point we move from imagined images to actual.

Inspector Gardet is in the card-index room. An elderly employee in a gray smock hands him back the note authorizing his investigation.

EMPLOYEE: The man you're checking is Stavisky, the dashing Sacha!

GARDET: Doesn't he go under the name Serge Alexandre now?

The Employee shrugs his shoulders, as though amazed at the extent of Gardet's ignorance. He goes over to a card file under the letter "A" and pulls it out. He takes out card and reads:

EMPLOYEE: "Alexandre, Serge. See Stavisky, Alexandre-Sacha, also known as 'Alex,' 'Jean-Sacha,' 'Doisy-le-Monty,' 'Victor Boitel.' Born November 20, 1886, in Slobodka, State of Kiev, Russia. . . ."

Gardet glances at the card file and hands it back to the Employee, who slips it back into its place and then turns to Gardet, who is saying:

GARDET: Which section has his file?

The old man chuckles.

EMPLOYEE: No section! It's a special file . . . kept under lock and key. No one can look at it without the express authorization of the chief himself.

Inspector Gardet finds what he has just heard hard to believe. But the old man, who seems to know much more than Gardet, laughs again, a high-pitched, rasping laugh.

EMPLOYEE: That's only the first of your surprises, Inspector. The first of many!

*

We see Inspector Gardet as he goes from office to office, on the trail of Serge Alexandre's police file. During his search we again hear his voice testifying before the commission.

GARDET (*voice over*): I finally tracked down the file I was looking for, when one of the functionaries told me that it was in Inspector Bonny's office. So I paid a visit to Chief Inspector Bonny, who in fact had the file. . . .

We see Gardet going into Bonny's office and speaking to him. We see Bonny laughing heartily, then getting up. He goes over and pulls out Alexandre's file, which he places on the table. He takes one document from it and shows it to Gardet.

GARDET (*voice over*): Bonny was thoroughly familiar with Alexandre's file. . . . He showed me a report dating from 1926 which already described him as a swindler, as the epitome of the type of person who lives by his wits. . . .

Bonny shoves the file, which is open, over toward Gardet. Gardet sees in it the cover of Le Petit Journal illustré *fancifully depicting the arrest at Marly-le-Roi.*

Gardet closes the file, looks at Bonny, and starts to say something to him.

*

But before we can hear Gardet's words, we find ourselves back in the committee room.

A deputy is asking Inspector Gardet a question.

DEPUTY: Did Inspector Bonny tell you why he had this particular file in his possession?

GARDET: No . . .

DEPUTY: Didn't it occur to you to ask him?

Gardet seems to hesitate for a moment. Then:

GARDET: No . . . I didn't have any special reason to ask him such a question.

*

We're back in Bonny's office. Gardet is just closing the file. He looks at Bonny, and this time we hear him say:

GARDET: And why are you so interested in this particular file, Bonny? Or should I phrase it differently . . . against whom do you intend to use Alexandre's file?

Bonny smiles, but there is something clearly cynical about it.

BONNY: That, my friend, will depend on certain circumstances. If the Right is returned to power, Alexandre's file will prove very useful in implicating the Radical-Socialists. . . . But if the Radicals retain power, I'll have the director of the *Sûreté* and the prefect of police in a pretty position. They're both involved up to their necks. You see, I'm playing Alexandre's little game: playing both ends against the middle. . . .

Gardet gives Bonny a long, hard look.

GARDET: You're playing with fire, Bonny! Don't get the idea into your head that you're untouchable!

    *

We're back again in the committee room. The deputies are listening to Inspector Gardet.

GARDET: Bonny, I assume, has also given a report. But if so I have no knowledge of it. I continued my investigation by paying a visit to the Place Saint-Georges.

    *

We see the scenes that Gardet's words evoke. The Inspector is next seen in the office building that houses Alexandre's many enterprises. He is talking to Alexandre's personal messenger, Laloy. During their conversation, Borelli comes in.

GARDET *(voice over)*: In the course of my investigation, I learned that Borelli was to be named head of the International Monetary and Development Fund. I also learned the names of the board of directors.

CHAIRMAN (*voice over*): And was Baron Raoul one of them?

GARDET (*voice over*): Yes, he was. I also paid a visit to the Claridge Hotel, to see if Stavisky was still registered there. . . .

We see Gardet in conversation with the hotel porter at the Claridge. Then he is seen walking through the lobby. Arlette, looking very elegant, emerges from the elevator and walks across the lobby to where a man whom Gardet has never seen before awaits her. It is Montalvo, who comes over and kisses her hand.

GARDET (*voice over*): I returned to the Sûreté and wrote up the results of my investigations for my superiors. Then I took it over to Monsieur de La Salle at the Ministry of Foreign Affairs. And that, Gentlemen, was the extent of my mission. . . .

During this last sentence, we see Gardet handing a report to Monsieur de La Salle, in an office of the Foreign Ministry. Monsieur de La Salle, a grizzled, distinguished-looking man whom we have seen previously in the antechamber of the committee room—the man who refused to acknowledge Baron Raoul's greeting there—glances at the report.

CHAIRMAN (*voice over*): What you are saying, Inspector, if I understand you correctly, is that as of November twenty-second, nineteen thirty-three, Foreign Affairs was fully aware of Alexandre's background, and who he really was?

Once again we are back in the room where the commission is holding its hearings.

GARDET: That is correct, Sir. . . .

DEPUTY: And what may I ask resulted from your report, Inspector? I mean, was there any follow-up?

GARDET: I don't know. On the judicial level, in any case, there was none. That was the last I heard of the matter.

44.

Baron Raoul's mansion in Paris. The time is noon, November 25, 1933.

Monsieur de La Salle is ringing Baron Raoul's doorbell. The door is finally opened, not by a servant, as one might expect, but by Baron Raoul himself. He is wearing a dressing gown, and is visibly surprised and somewhat embarrassed by the visit.

BARON RAOUL: De La Salle! What a pleasant surprise!

DE LA SALLE: I am here, Baron, on what I might term an unofficial visit. Can I come in for a few moments?

Baron Raoul is clearly trying to find an excuse not to let his visitor in, in all probability because he doesn't want him to see the dilapidated interior.

BARON RAOUL: It's Sunday . . . and all the servants have the day off . . . and I'm sorry to say my heating system's on the blink. . . .

But Monsieur de La Salle is not impressed by the Baron's complaint list, and goes on inside anyway.
Almost immediately, the door opens again. Monsieur de La Salle emerges, and the Baron accompanies him. They are standing on the top of the steps.

DE LA SALLE: My advice to you, Baron, is to resign from the board of directors. . . . I can tell you that the Foreign Ministry is not going to give its guarantee to the Hungarian debentures which form the financial basis of the Fund. . . .

But the Baron cuts him off.

BARON RAOUL: Listen, my friend . . . In any case, don't try to explain the set-up to me. I must confess that I don't understand the first thing about it. I agreed to serve on the board out of friendship. . . .

DE LA SALLE: A friendship I might categorize as most ill-advised, Raoul. Let me say it once again. Alexandre is not respectable.

First of all, he isn't even French. . . . He has no permanent residence. . . .

Both men are now standing next to the gate in front of the Baron's house.

45.

The Théâtre de l'Empire in Paris. The time is 10:15 p.m., November 25, 1933.

Alexandre is literally shaking with laughter.

ALEXANDRE: I'm not even French! Now how do you like that! And I have no permanent residence! For these gentlemen from the Foreign Office, anyone who hasn't owned his own home for the past five generations has to be considered a bohemian!

Alexandre, who seems completely relaxed, shakes his head and laughs again good-humoredly.

The camera moves back to reveal Alexandre and Baron Raoul, both in tuxedos, standing in the lobby of the Théâtre de l'Empire. Alexandre is drinking mineral water, the Baron champagne. In the background we can hear from time to time snatches of music, from A Penny's Worth of Flowers.

Alexandre puts down his glass and takes a small billfold from his pocket, from which he begins extracting various papers.

ALEXANDRE: There's my identity card. My military papers . . .

He hands the papers to the Baron, who seems insulted by the gesture.

BARON RAOUL: Please, Sacha!

ALEXANDRE: No, go ahead. I insist. Take a good look at them. You can tell your friend de La Salle you checked them personally. . . .

Baron Raoul reluctantly yields and checks the papers, all verified and official looking, proving that the bearer is indeed one Serge Alexandre.

ALEXANDRE *(voice over)*: Would you also like to check the police records?

Obviously, Alexandre is joking, but even so he is skating on thin ice.
The Baron hands his identity papers back, and Alexandre puts them back into his pocket.

BARON RAOUL: I'm most embarrassed, Sacha. But still, if the Ministry of Foreign Affairs refuses to guarantee those debentures? . . .

For a fleeting moment, Alexandre's face reveals a trace of concern, but the cloud quickly passes and he is once again his old, self-assured self.

ALEXANDRE: I'm not worried. I'll speak to the minister myself. He's a friend of Véricourt. He'll come around in the end.

And with a broad smile he takes the Baron by the sleeve and leads him away.

46.

The Municipal Pawnshop in Bayonne. It is 4:00 p.m., December 22, 1933.

The afternoon is clear and cold. A short, slight, insignificant-looking man appears beneath the arcades, heading toward the Municipal Pawnshop. The man we see is the Bayonne town auditor.

From a viewpoint outside the Pawnshop building, we see the auditor arrive in Gauthier's office. The auditor is talking, Gauthier is listening.

Now we are in the office itself. Gauthier's expression is impassive, or perhaps indifferent. Or he may only be putting up a good front. Whichever, the auditor visibly doesn't appreciate Gauthier's attitude.

AUDITOR: The numbers on these bonds don't correspond to any in your books! Perhaps you'd be kind enough to tell me, Monsieur Gauthier, just what that means?

As he talks, the Auditor is waving a sheaf of papers in Gauthier's face, but despite this the latter remains apparently unshaken.

AUDITOR: All right, *I'll* tell you what it means, Monsieur Gauthier. It means the Bayonne bonds are phony. And that you, and you alone, have been issuing fraudulent bonds!

Finally, Gauthier decides to speak up.

GAUTHIER: If I were in your shoes, Sir, I would close my eyes. I'd forget the whole thing. It's too big. It will drag you down, ruin you. . . .

The Auditor can hardly believe his ears. He's obviously so thunderstruck by Gauthier's words that he's momentarily at a loss for words. Gauthier takes advantage to say:

GAUTHIER: This is Friday, Monsieur. Next Monday is Christmas. We're going into a long weekend. Don't do anything rash. Think about what I've just told you. Go and talk it over with the deputy mayor. . . .

But the Auditor has heard all he wants to hear. He gets to his feet, feverishly picks up his papers, and leaves the room, slamming the door behind him.

Gauthier remains seated, perhaps in a daze, or perhaps just trying to figure out what his next move ought to be.

47.

The Hôtel Claridge in Paris. The time is 6:00 p.m., December 22, 1933.

The scene is Alexandre's suite in the Claridge. In the living room are three men in tuxedos, sipping champagne: Alexandre, Baron Raoul, and Montalvo. They all seem happy and relaxed. Alexandre's smile, which is always winning, is particularly seductive tonight.

BARON RAOUL: What we need in this country is the kind of elections they have in Spain. Or even better: a national bloc which would rule without any chamber or senate, with

of course the help of the professional organizations. Honorable men, worthy veterans of the war who have proved their mettle, should be given the key posts of government. . . .

He turns to Alexandre.

BARON RAOUL: That, by the way, is the main thrust of the play we're going to see tonight.

Alexandre is in fine fettle.

ALEXANDRE: What? Shakespeare advocated a national bloc? Are you trying to imply that Shakespeare was a disciple of your friend Maurras?

BARON RAOUL: You haven't lost your taste for paradox, have you, Sacha? Nonetheless, the fact remains that Shakespeare's *Coriolanus* is a violent attack on the parliamentary system. . . .

As Baron Raoul says these words, the door leading to the bedroom opens. Arlette appears, looking more beautiful then ever.

She is wearing a sumptuous evening gown, with an ermine wrap thrown over her shoulders. Around her neck is the lovely antique necklace that Alexandre brought her as a present early one summer morning in Biarritz.

All three men greet her arrival with admiring looks. Baron Raoul is the first to rise and go over to meet her. He kisses her hand.

BARON RAOUL: Arlette! How lovely, that ermine wrap! You are the harbinger of winter, of the joys of long snowbound nights when friends can get together!

As the Baron is paying Arlette his somewhat precious compliment, Juan Montalvo leans quickly over to Alexandre, his glass of champagne still in his hand.

MONTALVO: All the arrangements have been made. Tomorrow I'm leaving for Madrid. . . . And a week later we'll be depositing a million pounds sterling in your Swiss account.

Montalvo's voice is as precise as it is discreet. The expression that comes over Alexandre's voice is visibly one of joy, but with

a trace of ruthlessness, for one who knows him. Montalvo's words, however, mean that he is really home free—saved in the nick of time. Both men touch glasses, then get up to greet Arlette, who is radiant as she walks over to them, escorted by Baron Raoul.

48.

Bayonne. The time is 6:15 p.m., December 22, 1933.

Gauthier, handcuffed, and flanked by two policeman, is being led out of the Municipal Pawnshop. He is ashen.

49.

The Comédie-Française in Paris. The time is 9:00 p.m., December 22, 1933.

Theater programs can be very useful things. Thus by looking at the program of the Comédie-Française for the evening of

December 22, 1933, we see that the company was performing
Shakespeare's Coriolanus, in René-Louis Pachaud's translation.
We also learn that, coincidentally, the role of Coriolanus was
played by Monsieur Alexandre (!), that of Sicinius by Denis
d'Inès, and that of Virgilia by Vera Korène.

Now that we have been thus instructed, the camera retreats to reveal Arlette, flanked by Baron Raoul and Montalvo,
in a box at the Comédie-Française. Arlette is resplendent in her
ermine wrap, which lies just back off her shoulders. Just behind
them sits Alexandre.

During this scene this box is all we shall see of the Comédie-
Française, this choice box at the theater in whose semi-darkness can be detected the faces, hands, and immaculate clothing
of the occupants.

But though we will not see the stage itself, we will hear the
words that emanate from it.

CORIOLANUS (*voice over*): . . .
This double worship,
Where one part does not disdain with cause, the other
Insult without all reason; where gentry, title, wisdom
Cannot conclude but by the yea and no
Of general ignorance,—it must omit
Real necessities, and give way the while
To unstable slightness . . .

*At this point in Coriolanus's impassioned speech, we hear
reactions from the audience: even without clearly hearing the
words we can tell from the murmurs and the outbursts of applause that those reacting approve of Coriolanus's position.*

CORIOLANUS (*voice over*):
. . . pluck out
The multitudinous tongue; let them not lick
The sweet which is their poison. Your dishonor
Mangles true judgment and bereaves the state
Of that integrity which should become 't . . .

*Suddenly the door of the box opens. A ray of light shines in.
Alexandre turns around and sees that it is Borelli, beckoning
to him in such a way that he knows it must be important.
Neither Baron Raoul nor Montalvo have noticed Borelli, but
Arlette has. She watches Alexandre get up and leave the box, and
her face suddenly clouds with a look of fear and anxiety.*

BORELLI: They've discovered the phony Bayonne bonds!
Gauthier's in prison! . . .

*Alexandre's face falls. One has the impression of a bottomless
pit having opened all of a sudden, into which Alexandre is falling. Not unlike Arlette's recurring dream.*

ALEXANDRE: Did he mention my name?

Borelli looks at Alexandre, his face impassive.

BORELLI: He will, just as surely as night follows day! . . .

Alexandre-the-resourceful, who always has some kind of answer to every situation, now seems at a loss. It is Borelli rather than he who takes things in hand.

BORELLI: I got in touch with both Grammont and Véricourt right away. They're coming to the Empire as soon as the show is over.

Alexandre stares vacantly at him: Why at the Empire? he seems to be asking. As if reading Alexandre's thoughts, Borelli says:

BORELLI: You mustn't go back to the Claridge.

Alexandre shakes his head automatically, as though he were reacting in a dream. An usherette appears, and in no uncertain terms shhs them: they are talking too loudly. Meanwhile, we hear the muffled tones of Coriolanus's tirade against the rabble.

CORIOLANUS (*voice over*):
 . . . in a rebellion,
 When what's not meet, but what must be, was law,
 Then were they chosen . . .

A further round of applause can be heard from the direction of the audience. Borelli pulls Alexandre away from the entrance to the box, where they had been standing.

BORELLI: Go on over to the office. There are some papers that have to be burned. . . . Meanwhile, I'm going to try and lay my hands on Inspector Boussaud. . . .

Alexandre shakes his head bewilderedly as he lets Borelli lead him away. As they walk along the corridor surrounding the boxes, followed by the critical eye of the usherette, we again hear the angry voice of Coriolanus.

CORIOLANUS (*voice over*):
 . . . in a better hour,
 Let what is meet be said is must be meet,
 And throw their power i' the dust.

Again, applause and raised voices emanate from the audience, approving Coriolanus's anti-parliamentarian words.

50.

The Place Saint-Georges. The time is 9:30 p.m., December 22, 1933.

Alexandre is stooping down, still in his evening clothes, poking some papers that he is burning in the fireplace in his office. He has taken a revolver from a drawer in his desk. As he straightens up, his eyes focus on the large photograph of Arlette that graces the mantelpiece.

51.

The Comédie-Française. The time is 9:45 p.m., December 22, 1933.

Arlette, obviously very upset and worried about Alexandre's precipitous departure, sits stiffly, her face masklike. Baron Raoul

and Montalvo sit watching the stage, seemingly oblivious to Arlette's concern.

52.

The Théâtre de l'Empire. Later that night.

In the administrative office of the Théâtre de l'Empire, Inspector Boussaud, Borelli, and Grammont, the lawyer, are gathered. Both Borelli and Boussaud seem composed, but Grammont is so nervous he can't sit still.

BOUSSAUD: You have three days ahead of you. Because of the long Christmas weekend, nothing's going to happen before next Tuesday. . . .

GRAMMONT: He *must* leave!

Boussaud nods approval.

BOUSSAUD: If we manage to cover up the scandal, he will only have gone away for a few days' holiday. . . . If we don't, it's better that he not be here. If he stays, he's liable to say anything and only make matters worse.

BORELLI: I'll make sure he leaves Paris. . . .

GRAMMONT: Where are you going to send him?

Borelli looks at Boussaud.

BORELLI: One of our employees has a house in the vicinity of Chamonix. . . .

Boussaud's face registers approval, and in all probability he is privy to the employee Borelli is referring to. But Grammont is very displeased at being kept out of the secret. In a dry voice, he says:

GRAMMONT: What's the employee's name?

It is, in fact, Inspector Boussaud who supplies it.

BOUSSAUD: Laloy, Alexandre's personal messenger. . . . He's someone we can, how shall I say, manipulate. He once had a brush with the law. . . .

53.

The Comédie-Française. Late evening, December 22, 1933.

The door to the box opens softly and Alexandre comes back in and sits down at the place he had left an hour or more before. Arlette turns to look at him and sees his ashen face. She reaches over and wipes a dark speck from Alexandre's face.

The final curtain has just come down on Coriolanus. *The house lights come back up, and we can hear the applause and the shouts of "bravo" echoing below.*

54.

The Théâtre de l'Empire. Later that night.

Boussaud, Borelli, and Grammont are all standing at the window of the administrative office, which overlooks the street.

From their viewpoint, we see Alexandre's black limousine pull up and stop. Arlette, Alexandre, and Baron Raoul get out, while the liveried chauffeur holds open the door for them.

GRAMMONT *(voice over)*: You've known him for a long time, Inspector. What do you think Alexandre is going to do?

The camera focuses now on Boussaud's face.

BOUSSAUD: I really don't know Serge Alexandre all that well. . . . I know a man named Sacha Stavisky, a small-time hood and con-man who could charm you out of your skin. A man who was my stool pigeon. A first-class forger. . . . Stavisky would run away with Arlette and start all over again somewhere else. But Alexandre? I haven't the faintest notion what he might do!

55.

The Théâtre de l'Empire. A short while later that same night.

We're in the same administrative office of the Théâtre de l'Empire, but now the three new arrivals are present. The way the people are arranged in the room suggests that two rival camps have already formed: on one side are Boussaud, Borelli, and Grammont. On the other, Arlette and Alexandre. And a little off to one side, all by himself and probably not knowing what he is doing here, is Baron Raoul.

Grammont is speaking, and his tone is dry and peremptory.

GRAMMONT: . . . I know it's not easy, Sacha. But you have to admit that you're mostly to blame. It isn't as though I hadn't warned you. . . . During these past few months you've managed your affairs abysmally. You ought to have stopped throwing your money out the window!

There is an ice bucket on the desk, with an open bottle of champagne in it. Alexandre picks up the bottle and pours himself a glass.

ALEXANDRE: I also ought to have stopped greasing all your palms. It's not as though you all didn't profit handsomely from my reckless abandon! And what about Véricourt? Isn't he coming? *Deputy* Véricourt. *I'm* the one who financed his election campaign last year. He's *my* deputy. And is this the way he thanks me when I need him: by not showing up?

At this point Borelli interrupts, and his voice is harsh and contemptuous. But who is it he is talking to? Who is his contempt aimed at?

BORELLI: We'll all drop you like a lead balloon, Alex. If anyone asks, we'll say we didn't know you, that we met you once or twice in some restaurant, but that we really didn't know who you were. Do you know what else we're going to say? We'll say that if you really think about it, what's so surprising about the whole affair? We'll say that people are never on their guard enough when it comes to foreigners, refugees, and Jews!

Alexandre is looking at Borelli intently as he makes this confession, then he bursts out laughing and turns to Baron Raoul.

ALEXANDRE: And what is your feeling, Baron? Do you agree with Borelli here?

The Baron shakes his head. He looks as though he didn't know what to think.

BARON RAOUL: I'm your friend, Sacha, no matter what happens. But you lied to me. I wish you hadn't.

He really looks distressed.

56.

The Théâtre de l'Empire. A little while later that same night.

A man is making his way through the dimly lighted corridors of the Théâtre de l'Empire, looking for the administrative office, which he seems unable to locate. At random he pushes open whatever doors he comes to, and finally emerges onto the empty stage. The man is Véricourt, the distinguished deputy Alexandre refers to as "his." His footsteps echo on the stage.

VÉRICOURT: Hello here? Anyone around?

We hear his voice echoing in the darkened auditorium. Then, a few seconds later, the door at the back of the auditorium opens and Borelli appears.

BORELLI: Over this way, Monsieur Véricourt!

57.

The Théâtre de l'Empire. A short while later that same night.

Back in the administrative office. Véricourt is standing, facing Alexandre. He has just pronounced his verdict.

VÉRICOURT: It's all over, Alexandre. The curtain's come down. . . . You have three days to get out. Go to Chamonix as Borelli suggests and wait there for my instructions.

Alexandre is not ready to give up all that easily.

ALEXANDRE: If I stay, Véricourt, I can turn the situation around. . . . One week from now I'll have a million pounds sterling in my hands.

But Véricourt cuts him off.

VÉRICOURT: In a week, if we let you do as you say, you'll have

every policeman in France on your trail!

Then Alexandre explodes in blind fury.

ALEXANDRE: You mean they'd dare blame me? Those same people who've eaten at my table, who cashed my checks, who agreed to sit on the boards of my companies . . . you mean to say they'd dare go after me? But they seem to forget who they're dealing with, they seem to forget that my name is Alexandre and I've got a few skeletons I can drag out of my closet, too!

By the end of his tirade, Alexandre is laughing, but it is a mad, angry laughter. His hand squeezes the glass he is holding with such force that it literally explodes in his grasp, and blood suddenly spurts out, covering his hand.

ARLETTE: Sacha!

She literally bounds across the room to him and throws her arms around him. She takes his wounded hand and brings it to her lips, stemming the flow of blood with her mouth.

A spot or two of blood has fallen onto Arlette's ermine wrap and stained it. Baron Raoul, as though he were unable to bear the sight of that blood, gets up and leaves the room.

Suddenly the screen is flooded with a series of shots.

In the first, we see Arlette, dressed all in black, widow's veils floating around her, walking through snow. She stumbles, and a gendarme reaches out to prevent her from falling.

Now Arlette, in widow's garb, is walking behind a hearse through the snow.

Snow, and then more snow. And then, though it is still white, it is no longer snow but the sheet that covers Alexandre's body in the Chamonix hospital.

58.

The Hôtel Claridge in Paris. The time is evening, December 24, 1933.

In the living room of Alexandre's suite at the Claridge, Arlette is conferring with the jewel expert and fence, Van Straaten.

Van Straaten has just handed Arlette a fat wad of banknotes. Then he puts all of Arlette's jewelry, which has been spread out on the table, in his briefcase.

VAN STRAATEN: I'm really very sorry, Arlette, but that's the best I can do. All my potential customers are away on Christmas vacation, in Monte Carlo and Saint Moritz. I'll get you the rest of the money in a few days.

Arlette makes no comment. She gets to her feet and accompanies Van Straaten to the door. Just as he is about to leave, he turns back to her, and in an altogether different tone says:

VAN STRAATEN: When you come to think of it, the mighty Alexandre is ending up the same way little Sacha began: it's the women who save his neck.

Arlette says nothing. Her face is a stonelike mask as she opens the door for Van Straaten and holds it for him as he edges his way out.

59.

A café in the vicinity of the Ternes district in Paris. Later that same night.

Alexandre is just pocketing the wad of banknotes that Arlette has given him. He has a strange smile on his face.

ALEXANDRE: It's only normal. He's having his little revenge. A month ago I took him for a pretty penny when he brought me the Rosenkrantz jewels!

The café in which they are sitting is decorated for Christmas eve with festive garlands.

ARLETTE: Don't go away without me, Sacha! Let's both go. . . . We can go to . . . to Venezuela, anywhere, I don't care.

He laughs, but there is something sad and unconvincing about it.

ALEXANDRE: That's an idea! Venezuela. We could open up a French restaurant. Or a little shop selling knickknacks and souvenirs: *Au Chic Parisien* . . . or if the going gets really tough I can trade on your charms. . . .

Arlette nestles up against him.

ARLETTE: If only we stay together, nothing can ever happen to you.

ALEXANDRE: We'll soon be back together. . . . Véricourt has promised me that he's going to work everything out.

Just then, Borelli and Laloy arrive.

BORELLI: The car's ready, Alex!

Alexandre gets up. For a long moment he looks at Arlette. Then he turns and leaves the café, followed by both men. Arlette sits there alone.

60.

The Hôtel Claridge in Paris. The time is 11:00 a.m., December 26, 1933.

We are in Alexandre's apartment in the Claridge. Inspector Bonny is going through it, opening closet doors, checking the drawers of all the furniture: everything is empty. Not a stitch of clothing is left, not even the tiniest scrap of paper.

Inspector Bonny even checks out the bathroom, which turns out to be the only room where something has been left behind. The weights and pulleys and all the other paraphernalia that Alexandre used to exercise with are still there where he left them. Bonny lifts a weight, tries one or two other machines, and laughs shortly, really to himself. He walks through the empty suite once again. When he re-emerges into the living room, he finds Inspector Boussaud, sitting in an easy chair watching him.

At that precise moment the door opens and a hotel em-

ployee comes in, carrying a vase filled with a magnificent bouquet of carnations.

With both police inspectors watching, he goes over and puts the vase in its customary place on the mantelpiece.

BONNY: Do you mind telling me just what that is?

HOTEL EMPLOYEE: Monsieur Alexandre's carnations . . .

We can see that the Hotel Employee is not overly fond of police inspectors. Bonny gives a wicked laugh as he says:

BONNY: Haven't you got the word? If Monsieur Alexandre ever comes back here, it'll be in handcuffs!

The Hotel Employee seems unimpressed. Bonny, seeing he is making no impression, signals for him to leave. The Hotel Employee turns and, with an air of almost solemn dignity, leaves the suite.

Bonny takes one of the carnations from the vase and puts it in his buttonhole.

BOUSSAUD: You pleased? Your time has finally come.

Bonny, with no air of self-consciousness, simply shrugs his shoulders in reply.

BOUSSAUD: I want you to keep something in mind, Bonny. For your own good, you'd better make a very prudent investigation. Do I make myself clear? You know the rules of the game: the Stavisky scandal must be a Republican scandal. . . . What's corrupt is the Club, all those government back-scratchers. So you can implicate all the deputies, the ministers, and secretaries, and sub-secretaries in the whole Left coalition. But under no circumstances, Bonny, are you to implicate us in it. . . .

Bonny breaks in with a smile.

BONNY: And what about the prefect of police? He too belongs to the Club, right? So at what point do I draw the line?

Boussaud's reply is almost a shout.

BOUSSAUD: You figure out for yourself where you draw the line, Bonny! But if you implicate either the prefecture or the *Sûreté*, we'll break you!

Both men stare at each other: hard, long looks.

61.

The Stavisky Commission in Paris. The time is 11:00 a.m., April 19, 1934.

Inspector Bonny is standing in the witness stand, testifying before the so-called Stavisky Commission.

BONNY: On January eighteenth the head of my department called me up to his office, and said to me that the director had specifically ordered me to cease all investigation. I was suspended from my functions on January twenty-fourth. . . .

DEPUTY: If I understand you correctly, Sir, you wrote up a report indicating the extent of relations between Monsieur Chiappe and Alexandre Stavisky . . . and then on the eighteenth you were withdrawn from the case, and six days later relieved of your functions. . . .

BONNY: That is correct, Sir.

DEPUTY: And if I can carry my deductions one step further, I can assume, can I not, that all it takes to be relieved of one's functions is a report involving Monsieur Chiappe?

That questions, posed by a Left deputy, provokes a certain reaction from various other members of the Commission.

BONNY: Speaking for myself, Gentlemen, in response to that last question, I can only say: no comment.

62.

The Stavisky Commission in Paris. The time is 11:15 a.m., April 19, 1934.

Baron Raoul arrives in the antechamber of the room where the Commission is holding its sessions. He takes off his coat, his hat, and hands over his cane to the Court Usher. One might think that he is arriving at his club or some place which he is wont to frequent. Actually, the Court Usher greets him as though he were a regular and valued customer.

COURT USHER: There will be a short wait, Baron. But only a few minutes, I'm sure. Inspector Bonny's testifying now.

The Baron nods and takes a seat. He glances around the room to see who are the other persons waiting there. Among them are the blackmailer Alexandre talked to one day in a dressing room of the Théâtre de l'Empire the previous July, Borelli, and Laloy.

The Baron takes his newspaper, which is either Le Matin *or* Excelsior, *both ultra-conservative.*

The headlines are all about the Stavisky scandal on the one hand, and on the other about the discovery that Trotsky has been living in Barbizon just outside Paris. Baron Raoul looks at a photo in the paper of Trotsky's house, the Ker Monique *that we have already seen. It is guarded by gendarmes, and swarming around the gate is a bevy of clamoring journalists.*

63.

Barbizon. The time is 11:30 a.m., April 19, 1934.

A cordon of gendarmes surround the Ker Monique, *while a small crowd of bystanders and curious onlookers crane their necks trying to get a glimpse of the house or its occupants. There are also a couple of press trucks, on top of which movie cameras are perched, with a member or two of their crew operating them.*

Michel Grandville and Erna Wolfgang are among those trying to gain access to the house, but they are turned back by the police. Michel leads Erna along a path he obviously knows; it puts them on another side of the property, which is surrounded by a high wall. But here there are no police.

Inside the house Inspector Gardet is standing in the entrance

hallway, talking to one of Trotsky's secretaries.

GARDET: While waiting for a country to grant Monsieur Trotsky
a visa, the Government has decided that he will be removed
from his present quarters and taken to some place more
than three hundred kilometers from Paris. . . .

*A door opens and Trotsky appepars, accompanied by Natalia.
His face is covered with shaving cream, which covers his famous
goatee. He listens, smiling, to Inspector Gardet's words.*

GARDET *(voice over)*: After the unfortunate events of February
sixth, the Government is making every effort to calm
troubled waters, as it were. Now, the consensus is that your
presence so close to the capital is tending to arouse the
extremists of both Left and Right. . . . I have been assigned
to accompany you to your new residence.

*Meanwhile, Michel Grandville and Erna Wolfgang have
climbed up on top of the wall around the* Ker Monique, *from*

which they have a clear view of the yard and house.

GRANDVILLE: So the decision has been made to expel Trotsky. And in my opinion the fate of Fascism is going to be settled here, on French soil. The only problem is, Trotsky won't be here to fight it. And without him, the forces that might have joined together will splinter and scatter. It's really crazy, but when you think of it, it's all Stavisky's fault.

ERNA WOLFGANG: I don't follow you.

GRANDVILLE: It's very simple. Without Stavisky, there would have been no February sixth. And without the Fascist uprising that day, which caused the Daladier government to fall, there would have been no Right Wing coalition in power. Without which, Trotsky wouldn't have been expelled from France. Therefore, without Stavisky . . .

64.

The Stavisky Commission, Paris. The time is 3:00 p.m., April 19, 1934.

Arlette is on the witness stand in the hearing room.

CHAIRMAN: You knew your husband's psychology, his frame of mind. Was he prone to suicide, would you say?

Arlette looks wan and pale, and she glances around the room. She makes an obvious effort to weigh the question carefully and answer it honestly.

ARLETTE: He had periods of depression which sometimes lasted for quite a long time.

CHAIRMAN: I take it you're implying that his suicide is not something that strikes you as impossible to imagine?

Arlette bends as though struck by an invisible blow. She has trouble keeping her feet.

A succession of shots: Arlette, snow, black widow-veils, her walk through the snow in Chamonix, revealing exhaustion; she

stumbles and almost falls.

Then we are back in the hearing room, our camera on Arlette in the witness box.

ARLETTE: When I first went to Chamonix, I was sure he had committed suicide. Since then, so many stories have been bruited about that . . . I no longer know what to think. . . .

Suddenly her tone changes.

ARLETTE: But they separated us. They took him away from me. They cut all the lines that made him want to live!

Arlette's voice still echoes over the following scene.

65.

A chalet in Chamonix on the top of a hill: Le Vieux Logis. *The time is noon, January 8, 1934.*

Alexandre is alone in a bedroom of Le Vieux Logis. *He hasn't shaved for several days. He is lying on the bed, which is covered with a litter of newspapers. Through the window we can see the countryside, completely covered with snow.*

All the newspapers, we can see, have front-page stories about him, with headlines emphasizing the massive police-search of which he is the object.

With infinite care, Alexandre is cutting out all the newspaper pictures of Arlette with a pair of scissors.

66.

The town of Chamonix. The time is noon, January 8, 1934.

Laloy, Alexandre's "faithful" employee, is walking through the streets of Chamonix. He is heading back up to Le Vieux Logis, carrying a package of supplies and an armful of newspapers.

Laloy goes into the kitchen of Le Vieux Logis, puts down the papers, and starts to unwrap the packages.

The door opens and Alexandre appears.

LALOY: It's me, boss! I bought a twelfth-cake: we'll draw straws to see who's king.

But Alexandre isn't interested in the cake. He snatches up the newspapers on the kitchen table and goes back into the bedroom.

Laloy watches him leave. He shrugs his shoulders, then takes from his shopping bag both the twelfth-cake and the gold-paper crown. As he is doing this, the door reopens and Alexandre comes back in, holding a newspaper in his hand. It is La Liberté, a paper Alexandre once owned.

ALEXANDRE: Oh, are they being self-righteous! It really looks good on them. . . .

He shows the paper to Laloy. The headlines, of course, are all about the Stavisky Affair.

ALEXANDRE: *La Liberté!* "Freedom"! Well, let me tell you, that "freedom" cost me a pretty penny! They didn't have quite so many scruples not so long ago, when they were only too happy to take my checks. . . .

LALOY: That's life, Monsieur Alexandre. We know life's not very pretty.

Alexandre looks at Laloy, and he rubs his hand over his cheek, as though an idea had suddenly hit him. He smiles, and a new vitality seems to infuse his expression: one has the impression that he has just made some important decision.

ALEXANDRE: Laloy, as soon as you catch your breath, I want you to go back down into town and buy two berths on the night train to Paris.

Laloy seems taken aback. He looks frightened.

LALOY: Paris? But, Monsieur Alexandre, Paris means prison!

Alexandre is his old self again: his old demons have taken over, and he paces the room, working out his plans, building a future.

ALEXANDRE: And what do you think I'm in here? Isn't this a prison? I'm going back to Paris. . . . Tomorrow morning I'm calling a press conference. I'll tell them the whole story, from A to Z. . . . It will make some pretty headlines, Laloy, that I can assure you!

He has a sudden idea, which strikes him as funny. With a laugh he says:

ALEXANDRE: I just had a brilliant idea. I'll make a radio address, a little fireside chat to the public, from the Eiffel Tower station. All France will hear what I have to say!

He's dreaming, and his dreams visibly make him happy. But Laloy's reaction is quite the opposite: he's terrified. He tries to interrupt Alexandre's raving:

LALOY: But Monsieur Véricourt . . .

Alexandre lets him go no further.

ALEXANDRE: Véricourt? We'll see what our friend Monsieur Véricourt is going to say!

And, in fact, we do, in the following scene.

67.

Véricourt's apartment in Paris. The time is 11:00 a.m., January 8, 1934.

Direct cut to Véricourt, who is on the telephone. Standing beside him is Alexandre's lawyer, Grammont.

VÉRICOURT: Is this the Minister's office? Ah, it's you, Sir. This is Véricourt. Yes, I have the information. Yes. Chamonix is the place all right. The telephone number there is 319. If he thinks he hasn't got a chance, he's capable of putting a bullet into his head. What? Yes, runs in the family, as you say. He's armed, of course. Good-bye, my friend. Keep me posted. And my best wishes to the Minister himself. . . .

Véricourt hangs up. He looks up at Grammont as if to say: Well, it's done.

68.

Chamonix. The time is 2:00 p.m., January 8, 1934.

An impressive array of police—both uniformed gendarmes and police inspectors in civilian clothes, begin to assemble in the area just below Le Vieux Logis.

One has the impression that the gendarmes are taking no real measures to conceal their presence.

Inside Le Vieux Logis, the meal is over. Alexandre and Laloy have pushed the dishes aside and are playing cards. Laloy is wearing the paper crown on his head: obviously, they have drawn to see who becomes king.

Since he made his decision to return to Paris and fight, Alexandre is a changed man: full of vitality.

ALEXANDRE: I've gotten out of scrapes just as bad as this one. When I dreamed up that Bayonne bond scheme, believe me my fortunes were at a pretty low ebb. . . .

LALOY: I must confess, Monsieur Alexandre, that I still don't understand how those Bayonne bonds worked.

Laloy glances surreptitiously at his watch. He is visibly ill at ease.

But Alexandre, his eyes shining as he thinks back to the whole mad Bayonne bond scheme, seems oblivious to Laloy's nervousness. He starts to explain the mechanisms whereby for several years he was able to bilk literally millions from the public.

ALEXANDRE: It's really so simple it's childish. What you do is issue two sets of identical bonds. There's the real bond, let's say, worth two hundred francs, and another, the phony one, which has the same number, duly signed and sealed, which we assign any amount to we decide on, depending on the circumstances: twenty thousand francs, a hundred thousand francs, a million. In other words, we were minting money. The State was me!

His little joke pleases him. Laloy gets to his feet, however, saying:

146

LALOY: I have to go down into town, Monsieur Alexandre. I have to pick up those tickets.

Alexandre watches him flitter nervously about the room. Then Laloy puts on his coat and leaves the chalet. He walks down a snowy path and passes a group of police, both uniformed and inspectors. He shows not the slightest surprise at their presence. As soon as Laloy has passed, the inspector presumably in charge of the operation makes an arm movement which clearly signifies: Let's go!

Alexandre is lying on his bed, in the same bedroom of the chalet we have seen before.

Outside, a dog suddenly begins to bark. Alexandre gets up and rushes over to the window. He sees the gendarmes and the police inspectors heading up the path toward the chalet.

He goes back to the bed and lies down, like an animal that knows it hasn't a chance.

We hear the sound of glass breaking. Heavy footsteps invade Le Vieux Logis.

Alexandre hurries over to the door and locks it. Beyond the door, we can hear the sound of several people, but they seem strangely unhurried. Then someone turns the doorknob from the other room. Alexandre watches the doorknob turning.

Suddenly a succession of rapid shots. A house in Montigny, under the pale sunlight of November: the house where his father committed suicide one day seven years before. The beach at Biarritz. A white ermine on the white snow. Baron Raoul coming to meet him in the lobby of the Claridge. The limousine, as in Arlette's dream, descending the gray slopes. In short, the scenes of his life.

Two gendarmes are standing guard outside the chalet.
Suddenly we hear a shot. The gendarmes rush inside.

69.

The Petite-Roquette prison in Paris. The time is 3:00 p.m., April 19, 1934.

The Hispano-Suiza is seen, just like in the good old days. Inside are Montalvo and Baron Raoul. Both watch as the chaffeur

148

carries an enormous open basket of superb white flowers toward the gate of the Petite-Roquette, where Arlette is imprisoned.

MONTALVO: Arlette in prison . . . and all the guilty parties running around free! That, my friend, is the real scandal!

BARON RAOUL: They want to keep her in prison until the trial . . . to keep her from talking. They're under the mistaken impression that she knows Alexandre's secrets.

Baron watches the basket of flowers borne toward the prison; then his gaze fixes on the wall itself.

BARON RAOUL: Alexandre's secret . . . his only real secret . . . was Arlette. . . .

Now, in a low voice, he begins to recite:

BARON RAOUL: "What I shall like about death is its sheer laziness, the slightly dense and sluggish fluidity of death which, when you come right down to it, means that there are no dead but only those who have drowned. . . ."

MONTALVO: What in the world are you talking about?

BARON RAOUL: Nothing. About the Ghost in Giraudoux's *Intermezzo*. Alexandre's finest role. Ah, I can just imagine his laughter if he were to come back among us, if he were to see the passions that his whole adventure has unleashed. . . .

The chauffeur, who had disappeared through the prison gate, reappears, still carrying the basket of flowers, which the prison authorities have refused to accept. Not knowing what to do with them the chauffeur sets the basket down in front of the prison gate.
Meanwhile, Baron Raoul's voice can be heard saying:

BARON RAOUL *(voice over)*: I realized it too late, but Stavisky was announcing death to us. . . . Not only his own, not only those of this past February, but the death of an era, of a whole period of history. . . .

The Baron's voice trails off over a shot of Alexandre lying on the floor of the bedroom in Le Vieux Logis, *covered with blood.*

INTERVIEW WITH ALAIN RESNAIS

by Richard Seaver

Wherever Alain Resnais's *Stavisky* . . . has opened outside the director's native France, it has been received with generally rave reviews and excellent public reaction. In France itself, although the film had perhaps the best box office of any Resnais film, it was received with mixed reviews. We asked the director of *Hiroshima, Mon Amour* and *Last Year at Marienbad* if he knew any reason for this disparity.

RESNAIS: I think the answer is really very simple. In France the name "Stavisky" still evoked memories for many people. Even though the scandal went back forty years, there are a great number of people who still react emotionally to the name, who perhaps were hurt financially by the affair, who were involved politically on one side or the other. For them, any film on Stavisky would have to deal with the realities of the affair, present the facts as they occurred.

Q.: Didn't you present the facts?

RESNAIS: Any film is a fiction, as least for me. Unless of course one sets out to make a documentary, such as Jean-Michel Charrier made on the same subject for French television. That was an excellent documentary, but its concept and goal were totally different from ours. Going on the premise that the length of a film is from an hour and a half to two hours, it is absolutely absurd to think that in that space of time one can properly present the historical reality of such a complex event. This said, the facts in our *Stavisky* . . . are all historically exact, so far as I know. But they were the bases for our "fiction," points of departure rather than ends in themselves.

Q.: If your film was so clearly fiction, why did Stavisky's son try to get an injunction against it?

RESNAIS: On the grounds that it was defamatory, that it slandered his mother's name.

Q.: Arlette Stavisky is still alive?

RESNAIS: I believe so. In fact, I seem to remember that she's living in America.

Q.: I take it the injunction was not granted.

RESNAIS: No. In fact, the tribunal stated that, far from defaming the Stavisky name, the film constituted "a veritable rehabilitation" of that admittedly dubious character.

Q.: Was that your intent—to rehabilitate Stavisky?

RESNAIS: Not really. Neither Semprun nor I set out to whitewash Stavisky, any more than we wanted to blacken his name. What did interest us was the man's personality: on one hand, an enormous generosity, a theatricality, a strong life impulse; and on the other, an almost inexorable thrust toward death. I have always been interested in the functioning of the human brain. Especially when there seem to be two very contradictory impulses warring within the same mind, as in the case of Serge Alexandre. But the period, the historical situation in which Stavisky lived also fascinated us: there were clearly strong parallels between his time and our own. It was a time of political instability, a time when societies were living beyond their means. We were also interested in exploring the mechanisms of that society, how it "uses" at the same time as it is being "used." Stavisky took good advantage of his opportunities, but the world in which he operated flattered and encouraged him, until such time as it judged he had exceeded the limits, at which point it coldly suppressed him.

Q.: You're implying he was murdered by the police sent to capture him in Chamonix?

RESNAIS: Whether Stavisky was shot by the police or killed himself remains unsolved to this day. What we do know is that when the police went up to the *Vieux Logis* they made no effort to conceal their presence. It's a small, three-bedroom chalet, with a cellar beneath—

Q.: Is that the real *Vieux Logis* we see in the film?

RESNAIS: Absolutely, with its little red curtains that you see and say to yourself, You can't use those, they're too red to be true. But the fact is, when reality has the air of a stage set, it doesn't bother me to use it, as in this case. . . . But about the question of murder, the police took a good hour to search this rather small house, during which time Stavisky was locked in one of the bedrooms. They knew full well he was suicidally inclined. So whether Sacha put the bullet in his head or the police did seems rather academic: either way, it's murder. What was more, after he was shot, they waited two full hours before taking him to the hospital. There are those who maintain that if he had been taken immediately, he might have been saved.

Q.: The point being that under no circumstances was he to be saved, simply because he knew too much.

RESNAIS: That's the clear implication, and the basis for much of the resulting scandal. Cover-up: it's not a new story.

Q.: Before you made this film, what did the name "Stavisky" mean to you?

RESNAIS: What a child of twelve remembers from having followed the story in the papers and magazines, from having read them, much as you read a several-part serial.

Q.: I seem to remember your once having declared that you were incapable of making a "historical" film, one that requires reconstituting the past in any way. And yet with *Stavisky* . . . you have, for it is nonetheless a film of the thirties.

RESNAIS: The problem for me in making a film that isn't contemporary is that it seems to call for a suspension of disbelief. The creation of an illusion you know is false. But Semprun and I were in agreement right from the start that *Stavisky* . . . would be an anti-illusionist film.

Q.: By which you mean?

RESNAIS: Simply that we didn't for one moment set out to try and make people believe that, since we were using actors, they were anything *but* actors. I was, I won't say inspired by, but certainly had in the back of my mind, the way in which Sacha Guitry played Louis XV—or Louis XIV or XVI. He always made the spectator aware that it was he—Sacha Guitry—playing the king.

Q.: Could you tell us a little about the genesis of the project? Whose idea was it to make a film on Stavisky? Was it yours?

RESNAIS: No. I was in the States at the time. Semprun and his producer had talked about the idea, but in a vague way. When I came back to Paris, Semprun and I had dinner one night, during which we brought each other up to date. Semprun of course had already written one film I made, *La guerre est finie,* and had said that he wanted to be the first writer to collaborate a second time with me. He mentioned Stavisky as a possible future project that he might do after he had finished the two films he was working on—one his own documentary on Spain, and the other entitled *L'Attentat (Attempted Murder),* another rather documentary film on the kidnapping of Ben Barka. But I don't think he had me in mind as a director at that point. Since, however, no director had been decided on, I told him the subject intrigued me, so long as it was clear we would treat it as fiction.

When a few days later Semprun's agent, Gérard Lebovici, called me to ask if I was serious about directing the Stavisky, I told him I was, but reiterated my concerns about any historical film. If Jorge could give me a short first draft, I said, I could get a much better idea whether or not it was feasible. As soon as he did, I knew it was something I could do.

Q.: I note that the French edition of the script published by Gallimard bears the title *Alain Resnais's Stavisky.* Does that mean that you wrote the script with Semprun, or that it's more yours than his?

RESNAIS: Not at all. That's Jorge's way of saying, I suppose, the vision was mine, if you will. But I've never, never written a script, nor provided a subject. What I can bring is a kind of abstract form, a structure.

Q.: How long was it from the time you saw the first draft until you had a finished script?

RESNAIS *(laughing)*:About a year. Jorge had figured he could write it in about three months, but I knew that was unrealistic, for several reasons. For one thing he badly underestimated the editing time he would need on his own film, *Les deux memoires (Two Memories).* He expected to be finished in a couple of weeks. And for months I would receive phone calls from Jorge, from the editing room, saying, "I'm still here, but we should be finished next Sunday. Let's meet on Monday." Then Monday, another call, "I'm still here, Alain, but it should be only a few more days." Also, I mentioned that however much the film is fiction it is grounded in strict reality. There are about ten books on the Stavisky affair, all of which we read and assimilated. The best of them from our point of view was Joseph Kessel's *Stavisky, l'homme que j'ai connu,* published in 1934 at the height of the scandal. Kessel had known Stavisky, and unlike most of his contemporaries who, as soon as the bubble burst, acted as though they had never laid eyes on the man, had the courage to come out and paint a fair portrait. "I knew him, I wined and dined with him," Kessel proclaimed, adding, "and for those whose memories are short I would like to remind the world that Sacha Stavisky was an uncommonly charming man." I might add, parenthetically, that after the script was finished we showed it to Kessel, to see whether he felt we had been unfair in any way to the subject, and his response was: "That's it, that's the way he was. You've really captured the essence of the man." And while most of the press and some professional colleagues raised their eyebrows over our choice of Belmondo to play the lead, when Kessel heard it he said: "An excellent choice."

Q.: What about the commission's records? Did you use them for source material?

RESNAIS: Oh, yes. Semprun steeped himself in them, and considering the thousands of pages involved, it is understandable why it took longer to write the script than we had envisaged.

Q.: You mentioned Belmondo. How did you decide on him?

RESNAIS: The same way I try to decide on all my actors. I have a mental file of the possibilities for each part. Then when I have a finished script I read each scene trying to visualize who among them best works for it. Then I add up the totals. In the case of Stavisky, the Belmondo total was overwhelming.

Q.: What was his reaction when you contacted him about it?

RESNAIS: Cautious. I might say understandably cautious.

Q.: Why?

RESNAIS: For the simple reason that Belmondo is undoubtedly the most sought-after actor in France. He must receive two or three scripts a day. So he is naturally wary. "Does Resnais want me because he thinks I'm the best person for the role, or because of what my name will mean to the film?" But the fact is, he was the actor I wanted.

Q. What about the fact of using a "name" actor?

RESNAIS: That doesn't bother me. In fact, since we were dealing with a public figure—Stavisky—the notion of superimposing another public figure—Belmondo—rather intrigued me. But once having settled on that concept, I wanted to buttress his presence with other "name" actors. I feel it's better to have all unknowns or the contrary, that is if you have Belmondo, then it makes sense to have Charles Boyer and François Périer, for example. It's in a way less shocking, more natural.

Q.: How did you get Boyer?

RESNAIS: I've always wanted to do a film with Boyer, whom I greatly admire. In fact, Semprun said, "All Resnais wants to do is make a film starring Belmondo and Boyer, with music by Stephen Sondheim. He couldn't care less what the subject is, so long as he has those three elements in it." He's exaggerating of course, but there's a kernel of truth there. . . . In any case, Boyer is semi-retired, living in Switzerland. But when I contacted him he agreed to come to Paris to discuss the project. I spent three hours trying to convince him, and as you see I succeeded.

Q.: Admirably. His is a major contribution. Was that your first meeting with Boyer?

RESNAIS: No, years before I made a documentary called *Toute la memoire du monde*, about the French National Library, and I wanted him to do the narration. As it turned out, agents and lawyers got into the picture, and he never did it. But he remembered our 1956 meeting very well.

Q.: How about François Périer? He certainly has to rank as one of France's leading actors. How did you persuade him to play Borelli?

RESNAIS: Périer is a great actor, and I was very lucky to have him in that role. With him it wasn't a question of persuading; he *wanted* the part. It's all the more remarkable because when you read the script Borelli seems to be a non-role. But he read and liked the script, and that was enough. I've found, at least in Europe, that when actors really like a film, or a part, they'll do almost anything to play in it. I warned Périer that it was a tough role: "You're going to be in the picture virtually from start to finish, with almost no speaking part." But he didn't care. He sensed what he could do with the role, too, and in fact he comes off as very important. Moreover, for me his presence—again a known face—helped counterbalance the presence of Belmondo.

Q.: And Anny Duperey?

Resnais: I remembered her in Godard's *Deux ou trois choses que je sais d'elle*, where I thought she was very good. Then I went to see her in a play, Molière's *The Misanthrope*. Her Célimène impressed me greatly, especially the way she could magnetize the public. It was a matinee, and the theater was filled with school kids who were not exactly models of decorum. But whenever they would begin to get out of hand she would turn a withering gaze out at them, and within seconds the theater would be totally quiet. Arlette was a beautiful, liberated, magnetic personality—anyone who could mesmerize Stavisky had to be magnetic—and Anny Duperey struck me as perfect for the role.

Q.: Speaking of mesmerizing, one senses that you, or Semprun, or doubtless both of you, were rather mesmerized by your subject.

Resnais: By the subject matter, or the person of Stavisky?

Q.: By Stavisky himself.

Resnais: No question. It's not as though we planned it that way, however. I think what intrigued both Jorge and me initially was what I might term the "mechanism of fraud," how it worked and how society, including some of its most powerful—and presumably upstanding—members, could not only condone it but become deeply and inextricably involved in it. The deeper we went into it the more I found myself captivated by the character. Originally Stavisky did not occupy as preponderant a place in the script as he ultimately did. His proliferation in the film happened naturally, and in a way might be considered the cinematic equivalent of what had happened forty years earlier in Stavisky's life. The fact is, neither Semprun nor I were able to resist Stavisky's charm, and if we have been criticized for making him too "sympathetic," can't it also be looked on as the same kind of "fraud" he perpetrated so well in reality? In any case, since it did happen organically, we thought we ought to respect it.

Q.: Was that the major criticism of the film in France?

RESNAIS: That, plus the fact that we hadn't dealt with the heart of the matter, namely the scandal itself. For most French people the Stavisky affair begins where our film ends, that is with Stavisky's death. What they wanted to see were the repercussions, the riots on the Place de la Concorde, the behind-the-scenes political intrigues trying to keep the government from falling, the attempt of the Right to capitalize on the situation. All of which is of course a totally different film, which I'm incapable of making.

Q.: Speaking of politics, where did the idea of juxtaposing the Trotsky subplot originate?

RESNAIS: We were looking for a subplot, parallel plot, call it what you will, which would help situate the time and the world in which Stavisky's actions were taking place. We considered any number of possibilities—we could have used Mistinguett or Maurice Chevalier, to name but two—and Semprun came up with the Trotsky idea. Semprun's novel *The Second Death of Ramon Mercader* dealt with Trotsky in exile, so he was especially familiar with the details of Trotsky's sojourn in France, which coincided with Stavisky's rise and fall. But even so it was only one among several possibilities until one day, in reading the investigative commission's report—as Semprun says, "in volume 6, on page 4749 to be exact"—Jorge discovered that a Chief Inspector Gagneux of the *Sûreté*, who in December 1933 had been urgently requested by the Ministry of Foreign Affairs to make a thorough report on one Serge Alexandre, alias Sacha Stavisky, was the same man who had been assigned to keep a close watch on Trotsky during part of his stay in France. That was the link that clinched it, and Gagneux became our Inspector Gardet. But there were other buttressing parallels that we liked: both Trotsky and Stavisky were Russian Jews; both were, in different ways, exiles; both magnetic; both lost. In the eyes of the French, both were "métèques"—lousy foreigners—and one of the feelings we were trying to convey—and which the Trotsky subplot helped illustrate—was the scope and depth of xenophobia then prevalent in France. In the thirties, the French seemed convinced that whatever misfortunes they were suffering could be blamed on outside forces and influences. The two most common prejudices were anti-Semitism on one hand and anglophobia on the other. I think Ophuls' *The Sorrow and the Pity* was the first post-war film to document forcefully the depth of that double-prejudice. If the Germans "succeeded," if one can use the term, so well in their Occupation of France, it was because so many French people felt that way. After Dunkirk, the average Frenchman figured that between the German "enemy" and the English "enemy" there was really very little choice. And if in the waning days of Stavisky's life the Trotskys and the Erna Wolfgangs could still find refuge in France, the threads of the future were beginning to come together, and the brutal truth to which Borelli gives voice at the Théâtre de l'Empire, toward the end of the film, is what lay in the hearts and minds of most French people at the time.

Q.: Is Baron Raoul the spokesman of that sentiment?

RESNAIS: In a sense, because it is also true that most of the people who had those admittedly base feelings were not really evil, or bad. I remember a cousin of mine, a decent, well-meaning Breton, who in 1949 or '50, when he learned that I was breaking into films, came up to me and said, with a comforting air: "I really feel sorry for you. I know how hard it must be for you to break into the movie business." I asked him what he meant. "Well," he said, "with all those Jews who control everything, it must be impossible to break in." And when I said to him: "Thank God for the Jewish producers, without whom it would be impossible for me to break through," I suspect he thought I had lost my marbles. And my cousin, I hasten to repeat, was not a bad man: simply ignorant. . . . But to come back to Raoul, he is obviously a composite portrait, at once the symbol of French smugness and also the typical kind of person that Stavisky loved to have around him: impeccable credentials and lineage, perhaps dubious motives and reasons for orbiting in Stavisky's circle, but ultimately the epitome of respectability.

Also the symbol of the person who is overwhelmed by circumstances, who understands only imperfectly what is happening to him.

Q.: Earlier you mentioned Stephen Sondheim. Can we talk a little about the music? How you decided on Sondheim, and why?

RESNAIS: That's a question the film's producer, Alexandre Mnouchkine, asked me more than once: "Alain, why make things more complicated than they already are? Why do you have to have an American composer for a French film? And, to boot, someone who has never written any music for films before?"

I knew all Sondheim's music, but the deeper I got into the Stavisky, the more I knew his music was perfect. I remembered in particular one scene in *Follies* that has always remained with me: a scene that begins in gaiety and high spirits, with John McMartin in white tuxedo and top hat singing and dancing, a scene full of joy and hope, when all of a sudden the music deteriorates, the lighting turns funereal, the girls collapse and dissolve, and he, McMartin, can no longer remember the words or music. It's devastating, a scene I've never forgotten. The worm in the apple, death in the midst of life. For essentially that's the story of Stavisky: a man condemned to death, fully aware of it, yet madly in love with life. In the middle of preparing the shooting script I picked up the phone from Paris and called Sondheim in New York.

Q.: Had you ever met him?

RESNAIS: An innocuous meeting, arranged by mutual friends. He invited me to his house for tea one afternoon, and we exchanged compliments.

Q.: How did the transatlantic phone conversation go?

RESNAIS: Something like this:

RESNAIS: (*after explaining briefly the gist of the movie's subject*): Actually, I can't conceive of any other composer's music working for this film. Shall I send you a script?

SONDHEIM: You know, I've never done the music for a film. Doesn't that bother you?

RESNAIS: Not in the least. What worries me is that you won't have the time to do it.

SONDHEIM: I'll take the time.

RESNAIS: What also worries me is that when lawyers and agents get into the act we'll never reach an agreement.

SONDHEIM: If it's money you're worried about, believe me it won't be a problem.

To give you an idea how important Sondheim's music was to me, when writing the shooting script I conceived certain key scenes rhythmically, in terms of his music. And on the first day of shooting, I had my tape recorder handy, with key passages of *A Little Night Music* constantly in my ear, to make sure that the rhythm of the scene coincided with Sondheim's music. That involved the speed with which the actors walked, Baron Raoul's gestures, the whole scene with the white airplane outside Biarritz.

Q.: Can we talk about technique for a moment? Some American critics have compared *Stavisky* to *The Great Gatsby* —I realize the comparison is superficial—and found that you captured the feel of the time the way *Gatsby* didn't. Forgetting the comparison, one does get from Stavisky a real feeling of the thirties, and especially of the films of the thirties. How did you achieve that feeling?

RESNAIS: I decided from the outset that we would make *Stavisky* . . . , from a technical viewpoint, as though it were being made in the thirties. By that I mean that our setups and our shot angles would be those that, technically, could have been made with equipment available to thirties' directors. With the colors, too: I felt that to convey the feeling of 1934 I couldn't use realistic 1974 colors. Sacha Vierny [director of photography] and I decided to take the risk—and it was a calculated risk—to try to simulate the style and colors of the Pathéorama films of the thirties, limit ourselves to a minimum of colors. Ideally we would have liked to make a bichrome film, that is one in which the only two colors would have been dark brown and red. That proved technically impossible, but we nonetheless worked in that direction. What we also did was steep ourselves in the pictorial magazines of the period, which helped us orient our characters' pace and positions. By the way, the issue of the *Petit Journal* you see in the picture, the one whose cover depicts Stavisky's arrest at Marly, is the actual 1926 issue. And, obviously, our filmed depictions of that scene and Sacha's arrest were influenced by those thirties' graphics.

Q.: Are colors symbolic for you? One can't help remarking the almost postcard summer warmth of the opening scene, moving to the browns and grays of fall at Barbizon and the deathly white of Chamonix. But the colors red, black, and white predominate.

RESNAIS: Their use is intentional, of course, though my goal is to make them unobtrusive. What I am striving for in a film is to try to construct a kind of compact object in which all the pieces or elements interrelate, but in isolation seem irrational. What I'm trying to create are different kinds of harmonics, which taken together will make an emotional impact.

Q.: One final question: could you tell us what the small stone pyramid is that recurs, I believe, twice in the film?

RESNAIS: It's one of those irrational but not meaningless elements I just mentioned. The pyramid is located in the Parc Monceau in Paris, and no one, including the guidebooks, seems to be able to account for its origin. All they seem to know is that it was there as early as the eighteenth century. Then too, Stavisky lived near the Parc Monceau—another irrational but interesting coincidence, and as Dr. Mézy notes at one point, Alexandre's youth is full of mysteries. So one can dream of the young Sacha walking in the park, passing that mysterious pyramid. . . . Apropos that monument, I might mention an amusing anecdote about it. I always put a bit more in my shooting scripts than I know I'll need, figuring I can always eliminate. This monument was one of those elements I included without being sure we'd ever use it. But when the day came to shoot it we went to the Parc Monceau—the whole crew, seventeen in all, as I remember, with equipment trucks trailing behind—and as we started walking through the park one of the crew said, "Where is it, Alain?" And suddenly I hadn't the faintest idea where it was, or whether it was really even in the Parc Monceau. And then the thought crossed my mind: maybe it's not even in Paris, that monument; maybe it's in a park in Rome I visited years ago. But I bravely kept walking, beginning however to sweat. And just as I was about to give up and confess, we turned a corner and there it was.

But to answer your question: there's something funereal about that pyramid, and *Stavisky* is ultimately about death. And there is as well, as I suggested, something mysterious and enigmatic about it, just as the life—and death—of Stavisky were mysterious and enigmatic.

Translated by S.D.